John Nichols

Six Old Plays On Which Shakespeare Founded his Measure for

Mearsure, Comedy of Errors...

Volume II

John Nichols

Six Old Plays On Which Shakespeare Founded his Measure for Mearsure, Comedy of Errors...
Volume II

ISBN/EAN: 9783337067571

Printed in Europe, USA, Canada, Australia, Japan

Cover: Foto ©Andreas Hilbeck / pixelio.de

More available books at **www.hansebooks.com**

SIX
OLD PLAYS,

ON WHICH

SHAKSPEARE

FOUNDED HIS

MEASURE FOR MEASURE.
COMEDY OF ERRORS.
TAMING THE SHREW.
KING JOHN.
K. HENRY IV. AND K. HENRY V.
KING LEAR.

IN TWO VOLUMES.

VOLUME II.

LONDON,

Printed for S. LEACROFT, Charing-Crofs:
And fold by J. NICHOLS, Red-Lion Paffage, Fleet-ftreet;
T. EVANS, in the Strand; and H. PAYNE, Pall Mall.

MDCCLXXIX.

OLD PLAYS.

VOLUME THE SECOND.

CONTAINING

THE TROUBLESOME REIGN OF K. JOHN.

THE FAMOUS VICTORIES OF HENRY V.

THE TRUE CHRONICLE HISTORY OF KING LEIR,
AND HIS THREE DAUGHTERS, GONORILL,
RAGAN, AND CORDELLA.

✻ a 2

THE

SECOND PART

OF THE

Troublefome RAIGNE of

KING JOHN.

CONTAINING

The Entrance of LEWIS the *French* Kings Sonne:

WITH THE

Poyfoning of King JOHN by a Monke.

THE

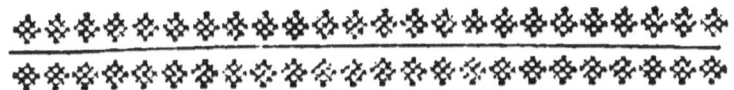

THE SECOND PART

OF THE TROUBLESOME

RAIGNE of KING JOHN.

CONTAINING

The Entrance of Lewis the *French* Kings Sonne:

WITH THE

Poyſoning of King John by a Monke.

Enter yong Arthur *on the walls.*

NOW help good hap to further mine entent,
Croſſe not my youth with any more extremes :
I venter life to gaine my libertie,
And if I die, worlds troubles have an end.
Feare gins diſſwade the ſtrength of my reſolve,
My holde will faile, and then alas I fall,
And if I fall, no queſtion death is next :
Better deſiſt, and live in priſon ſtill.
Priſon ſaid I ? nay, rather death than ſo :

Comfort

Comfort and courage come againe to me,
Ile venter fure : tis but a leape for life.

He leapes, and brufing his bones, after he was from his traunce,
fpeakes thus ;

Hoe, who is nigh ? fome bodie take me up.
Where is my mother ? let me fpeake with her.
Who hurts me thus ? fpeake hoe, where are you gone ?
Ay me poore *Arthur*, I am heere alone.
Why calld I mother, how did I forget ?
My fall, my fall, hath killd my mothers fonne.
How will fhe weepe at tidings of my death ?
My death indeed, O God, my bones are burft.
Sweete *Jefu* fave my foule, forgive my rafh attempt,
Comfort my mother, fhield her from defpaire,
When fhee fhall heare my tragycke overthrowe.
My heart controls the office of my tongue,
My vitall powers forfake my brufed trunke,
I die I die, heaven take my fleeting foule,
And lady mother all good hap to thee.   [*He dies.*

Enter Pembroke, Salifburie, Effex.

Effex.
My lords of *Pembroke* and of *Salifburie*,
We muft be carefull in our policie,
To undermine the keepers of this place,
Elfe fhall we never find the princes grave.
              Pembroke.
My lord of *Effex*, take no care for that,
I warrant you it was not clofely done.
But who is this ? lo lords the withered flowre,
Who in his life fhin'd like the mornings blufh,
Caft out a doore, deni'd his buriall right,
A prey for birds and beafts to gorge upon.
              Salifburie.
O ruthfull fpectacle ! O damned deed !
My finewes fhake, my very heart doth bleed.

                                    Effex.

Essex.

Leave childish teares brave lords of *England*,
If water-floods could fetch his life againe,
My eies should conduit forth a sea of teares.
If sobs would helpe, or forows serve the turne,
My heart should volley out deepe piercing plaints.
But bootelesse were't to breath as many sighes
As might eclipse the brightest sommers sunne,
Here rests the helpe, a service to his ghost.
Let not the tyrant causer of this dole,
Live to triumph in ruthfull massacres,
Give hard and heart, and *Englishmen* to armes,
Tis Gods decree to wreake us of these harmes.

Pembroke.

The best advice: but who comes posting here?

Enter Hubert.

Right noble lords, I speake unto you all,
The king entreats your soonest speed
To visit him, who on your present want,
Did ban and curse his birth, himselfe and me,
For executing of his strict command.
I saw his passion, and at fittest time,
Assur'd him of his cousins being safe,
Whom pity would not let me doe to death :
He craves your company my lords in haste,
To whom I will conduct young *Arthur* straight,
Who is in health under my custody.

Essex.

In health base villaine, were't not I leave the crime
To Gods revenge, to whom revenge belongs,
Here should'st thou perish on my rapiers point.
Call'st thou this health ? such health betide thy friends,
And all that are of thy condition.

Hubert.

My lords, but heare me speake, and kil me then,
If here I left not this yong prince alive,
Maugre the hastie edict of the king,
Who gave me charge to put out both his eyes,

That

5

That God that gave me living to this houre,
Thunder revenge upon me in this place:
And as I tendred him with earneſt love,
So God love me, and then I ſhall be we'l.
                    Saliſbury.
Hence traytor hence, thy counſel is herein.
                              [*Exit* Hubert.

Some in this place appointed by the king,
Have throwne him from this lodging here above,
And ſure the murther hath bin newly done,
For yet the body is not fully cold.
                    Eſſex.
    How ſay you lords, ſhal we with ſpeed diſpatch
Under our hands a packet into *France*,
To bid the *Dolphin* enter with his force,
To claime the kingdom for his proper right,
His title maketh lawfull ſtrength thereto.
Beſides, the Pope, on peril of his curſe,
Hath bard us of obedience unto *John*,
This hatefull murder, *Lewis* his true deſcent,
The holy charge that we receiv'd from *Rome*,
Are weightie reaſons, if you like my reed,
To make us all perſever in this deed.
                    Pembroke.
    My lord of *Eſſex*, well have you advis'd,
I will accord to further you in this.
                    Saliſbury.
    And *Saliſbury* will not gaineſay the ſame:
But aide that courſe as farre forth as he can.
                    Eſſex.
    Then each of us ſend ſtraight to his allies,
To win them to this famous enterpriſe:
And let us all yclad in palmers weed,
The tenth of *April* at S. *Edmunds Bury*
Meet to conferre, and on the altar there
Sweare ſecrecie and aid to this adviſe.
Meane while, let us convey this body hence,
And give him buriall, as befits his ſtate,
Keeping his months mind, and his obſequies
With ſolemne interceſſion for his ſoule.
How ſay you lordings, are you all agreed?
                              Pembroke.

Pembroke.

The tenth of *April* at S. *Edmunds Burie*,
God letting not, I will not faile the time.

Essex.

Then let us all convey the body hence.   [*Exeunt.*

Enter K. John, *with two or three, and the prophet.*

John.

Disturbed thoughts, foredoomers of mine ill,
Distracted passions, signes of growing harmes,
Strange prophecies of imminent mishaps,
Confound my wits, and dull my senses so,
That every object these mine eies behold,
Seeme instruments to bring me to my end.
Ascension day is come, *John* feare not then
The prodigies this pratling prophet threats.
'Tis come indeed : ah were it fully past,
Then were I carelesse of a thousand feares.
The diall tels me, it is twelve at noone.
Were twelve at midnight past, then might I vaunt,
False seers prophecies of no import.
Could I as well with this right hand of mine
Remove the sunne from our meridian,
Unto the moonciled circle of th' *antipodes*,
As turne this steele from twelve to twelve agen,
Then *John*, the date of fatall prophecies,
Should with the prophets life together end.
But *multa cadunt inter calicem suprémaque labra.*
Peter, unsay thy foolish doting dreame,
And by the crowne of *England* here I sweare,
To make thee great, and greatest of thy kin.

Peter.

King *John*, although the time I have prescrib'd
Be but twelve houres remaining yet behind,
Yet doe I know by inspiration,
Ere that fixt time be fully come about,
King *John* shall not be king as heretofore.

John.

Vaine, buzzard, what mischance can chance so soone,
To set a king beside his regall seat ?

My

My heart is good, my body paffing ftrong,
My land in peace, my enemies fubdu'd,
Onely my barons ftorme at *Arthurs* death,
But *Arthur* lives, I there the challenge growes,
Were he difpatch'd unto his longeft home,
Then were the king fecure of thoufand foes.
Hubert, what newes with thee, where are my lords?

             Hubert.

Hard newes my lord, *Arthur* the lovely prince,
Seeking to efcape over the caftle walles,
Fell headlong downe, and in the curfed fall
He brake his bones, and there before the gate
Your barons found him dead, and breathleffe quite.

             John.

Is *Arthur* dead? then *Hubert* without more wordes hang
    the prophet.
Away with *Peter*, villain out of my fight,
I am deafe, be gone, let him not fpeake a word.
Now *John*, thy feares are vanifht into fmoake,
Arthur is dead, thou guiltleffe of his death.
Sweet youth, but that I ftrived for a crowne,
I could have well affoarded to thine age,
Long life, and happineffe to thy content.

           Enter the Baftard.

             John.
Philip what newes with thee?
             Baftard.
The newes I heard was *Peters* prayers,
Who wifht like fortune to befall us all:
And with that word, the rope his lateft friend,
Kept him from falling headlong to the ground.
             John.
There let him hang, and be the ravens food,
While *John* triumphs in fpite of prophecies.
But whats the tydings from the popelings now?
What fay the monkes and priefts to our proceedings?
Or where's the barons that fo fuddainely
Did leave the king upon a falfe furmife?

                         Baftard.

Baſtard.
The prelates ſtorme and thirſt for ſharp revenge :
But pleaſe your majeſtie, were that the worſt,
Is little ſkild : a greater danger growes,
Which muſt be weeded out by carefull ſpeed,
Or all is loſt, for all is leveld at.

John.
More frights and feares! what ere thy tidings be,
I am prepar'd: then *Philip*, quickly ſay,
Meane they to murder, or impriſon me,
To give my crowne away to *Rome* or *France* ;
Or will they each of them become a king?
Worſe than I thinke it is, it cannot be.

Baſtard.
Not worſe my lord, but every whit as bad.
The nobles have elected *Lewis* king,
In right of lady *Blanch,* your neece, his wife :
His landing is expected every houre,
The nobles, commons, clergie, all eſtates,
Incited chiefly by the cardinall,
Pandulph that lies here legate for the Pope,
Thinke long to ſee their new elected king.
And for undoubted proofe, ſee here my liege,
Letters to me from your nobilitie,
To be a partie in this action :
Who under ſhew of ſained holineſſe,
Appoint their meeting at S. *Edmunds Burie.*
There to conſult, conſpire, and conclude
· The overthrowe and downefall of your ſtate.

John.
Why ſo it muſt be : one houre of content,
Match'd with a month of paſſionate effects.
Why ſhines the ſunne to favour this conſort ?
Why doe the winds not break their brazen gates,
And ſcatter all theſe perjur'd complices,
With all their counſels, and their damned drifts ?
But ſee the welkin rolleth gently on,
There's not a lowring cloud to frowne on them ;
The heaven, the earth, the ſunne, the moone and all,
Conſpire with thoſe confederates my decay.

Then

Then hell for me, if any power be there,
Forfake that place, and guide me ftep by ftep,
To poyfon, ftrangle, murder in their fteps
Thefe traytors: oh that name is too good for them,
And death is eafie: is there nothing worfe,
To wreake me on this proud peace-breaking crew?
What faift thou *Philip?* why affifts thou not?

> *Baftard.*

Thefe curfes (good my lord) fit not the feafon:
Help muft defcend from heaven againft this treafon?

> *John.*

Nay thou wilt prove a traytor with the reft,
Goe get thee to them, fhame come to you all.

> *Baftard.*

I would be loath to leave your highneffe thus,
Yet you command, and I, though griev'd, will goe.

> *John.*

Ah *Philip,* whither go'ft thou? come againe.

> *Baftard.*

My lord, thefe motions are as paffions of a mad man.

> *John.*

A mad man *Philip,* I am mad indeed,
My heart is maz'd, my fences all foredone.
And *John* of *England* now is quite undone.
Was ever king as I oppreft with cares?
Dame *Elianor* my noble mother queene,
My onely hope and comfort in diftreffe,
Is dead, and *England* excommunicate,
And I am interdicted by the pope,
All churches curft, their doores are fealed up,
And for the pleafure of the *Romifh* prieft,
The fervice of the higheft is neglected,
The multitude (a beaft of many heads)
Doe wifh confufion to their foveraigne:
The nobles blinded with ambitions fumes,
Affemble powers to beate mine empire downe,
And more than this, elect a forrein king.
O *England,* wert thou ever miferable,
King *John* of *England* fees thee miferable:
John, tis thy finnes that makes it miferable,

Quicquid

Quicquid delirunt Reges, plectuntur Achivi.
Philip, as thou haſt ever lov'd thy king,
So ſhow it now : poſt to S. *Edmunds Burie,*
Diſſemble with the nobles, know their drifts,
Confound their divelliſh plots, and damned deviſes.
Though *John* be faultie, yet let ſubjects beare,
He will amend, and right the peoples wrongs.
A mother though ſhee were unnaturall,
Is better than the kindeſt ſtep-dame is :
Let never *Engliſhman* truſt forraine rule.
Then *Philip* ſhew thy fealty to thy king,
And mongſt the nobles plead thou for the king.

                              Baſtard.
    I goe my lord : ſee how he is diſtraught,
This is the curſed prieſt of *Italy*
Hath heap'd theſe miſchiefes on this hapleſſe land.
Now *Philip,* hadſt thou *Tullies* eloquence,
Then might'ſt thou hope to plead with good ſucceſſe. [*Exit.*

                              John.
    And art thou gone ? ſucceſſe may follow thee :
Thus haſt thou ſhew'd thy kindneſſe to thy king.
Sirra, in haſte goe greet the cardinall,
Pandulph I meaue, the legat from the Pope.
Say that the king deſires to ſpeake with him.
Now *John* bethinke thee how thou maiſt reſolve ;
And if thou wilt continue *Englands* king,
Then caſt about to keepe thy diadem ;
For life and land, and all is leveld at.
The pope of *Rome,* tis he that is the cauſe,
He curſeth thee, he ſets thy ſubjects free
From due obedience to their ſoveraigne :
He animates the nobles in their warres,
He gives away the crowne to *Philips* ſonne,
And pardons all that ſeeke to murther thee :
And thus blind zeale is ſtill predominant.
Then *John* there is no way to keepe thy crowne,
But finely to diſſemble with the pope :
That hand that gave the wound muſt give the ſalve
To cure the hurt, elſe quite incurable.
Thy ſinnes are ſarre too great to be the man

                                        T'aboliſh

T'abolifh pope, and poperie from thy realme:
But in thy feate, if I may guefle at all,
A king fhall raigne that fhall fupprefle them all.
Peace *John*, here comes the legate of the pope,
Diflemble thou, and whatfoere thou fai'ft,
Yet with thy heart wifh their confufion.

Enter Pandulph.

Pandulph.
Now *John*, unworthy man to breath on earth,
That do'ft oppugne againft thy mother church:
Why am I fent for to thy curfed felfe?
John.
Thou man of God, vicegerent for the pope,
The holy vicar of S. *Peters* church,
Upon my knees, I pardon crave of thee,
And doe fubmit me to the fee of *Rome*,
And vow for penance of my high offence,
To take on me the holy croffe of Chrift,
And carry armes in holy chriftian warres.
Pandulph.
No *John*, thy crowching and diffembling thus
Cannot deceive the legate of the pope,
Say what thou wilt, I will not credite thee:
Thy crowne and kingdome both are tane away,
And thou art curft without redemption.
John.
Accurft indeede to kneele to fuch a drudge,
And get no help with thy fubmiffion,
Unfheathe thy fword, and fley the mifprowd prieft
That thus triumphs ore thee a mightie king:
No *John*, fubmit againe, diflemble yet,
For priefts and women muft be flattered.
Yet holy father thou thy felfe doft know,
No time too late for finners to repent,
Abfolve me then, and *John* doth fweare to do
The uttermoft what ever thou demaundft.
Pandulph.
John, now I fee thy hearty penitence,
I rew and pitty thy diftreft eftate,

One

One way is left to reconcile thy felfe,
And onely one which I fhall fhew to thee.
Thou mult furrender to the fee of *Rome*
Thy crowne and diadem, then fhall the pope
Defend thee from th'invafion of thy foes.
And where his holinefle hath kindled *Fraunce*,
And fet thy fubjects hearts at warre with thee,
Then fhall he curfe thy foes, and beate them downe,
That feeke the difcontentment of the king.

John.

From bad to worfe, or I mult loofe my realme,
Or give my crowne for penance unto *Rome :*
A miferie more piercing than the darts
That breake from burning exhalations power.
What, fhall I give my crowne with this right hand?
No: with this hand defend thy crowne and thee.
What newes with thee?

Enter Meffenger.

Pleafe it your majeftie, there is defcried on the coaft of
Kent an hundred fayle of fhips, which of all men is thought
to be the *French* fleet, under the conduct of the *Dolphin*, fo
that it puts the countrey in a mutiny, fo they fend to your
grace for fuccour.

K. John.

How now lord Cardinal, what's your beft advife?
Thefe mutinies muft be allaid in time,
By policy or headftrong rage at leaft.
O *John*, thefe troubles tyre thy wearied foule,
And like to *Luna* in a fad eclipfe,
So are thy thoughts and paffions for this newes.
Well may it be, when kings are grieved fo,
The vulgar fort worke princes overthrowe.

Cardinal.

K. *John*, for not effecting of thy plighted vow,
This ftrange annoyance happens to thy land :
But yet be reconcil'd unto the church,
And nothing fhall be grievous to thy ftate.

T   *John.*

John.

Oh *Pandulph*, be it as thou haft decreed,
John will not fpurne againft thy found advife,
Come lets away, and with thy helpe I trow,
My realme fhall flourifh, and my crowne in peace.

Enter the nobles, Pembrooke, Effex, Chefter, Bewchampe.
Clare, *with others.*

Pembrooke.

Now fweet S. *Edmund* holy faint in heaven,
Whofe fhrine is facred, high efteem'd on earth,
Infuze a conftant zeale in all our hearts,
To profecute this act of mickle weight,
Lord *Bewchampe* fay, what friends have you procur'd.

Bewchampe.

The L. *Fitz Water*, L. *Percie*, and L. *Roffe*,
Vow'd meeting here this day the leventh houre.

Effex.

Under the cloke of holy pilgrimage,
By that fame houre on warrant of their faith,
Philip Plantaginet, a bird of fwifteft wing,
Lord *Euftace*, *Vefcy*, lord *Creffy*, and lord *Mowbrey*,
Appointed meeting at S. *Edmunds* fhrine.

Pembrooke.

Untill their prefence, Ile conceale my tale,
Sweet complices in holy chriftian acts,
That venture for the purchaffe of renowne,
Thrice welcome to the league of high refolve,
That pawne their bodies for their foules regard.

Effex.

Now wanteth but the reft to end this worke,
In pilgrimes habite comes our holy troupe
A furlong hence, with fwift unwoonted pace,
May be they are the perfons you expect.

Pembrooke.

With fwift unwoonted gate, fee what a thing is zeale,
That fpurs them on with fervence to this fhrine,
Now joy come to them for their true intent:
And in good time, here come the war-men all,

That

That fweat in body by the minds difeafe :
Hap and harts-eafe brave lordings be your lot.

Enter the Baftard Philip, &c.

Amen my lords, the like betide your lucke,
And all that travell in a chriftian caufe.
Effex.
Cheerely repli'd brave branch of kingly ftocke,
A right *Plantagenet* fhould reafon fo.
But filence lords, attend our commings caufe :
The fervile yoke that pained us with toyle,
On ftrong inftinct hath fram'd this conventicle,
To eafe our necks of fervitudes contempt.
Should I not name the foeman of our reft,
Which of you all fo barren in conceipt,
As cannot levell at the man I meane ?
But left enigma's fhadow fhining truth,
Plainely to paint, as truth requires no art.
Th'effect of this refort importeth this,
To root and cleane extirpate tyrant *John,*
Tyrant I fay, appealing to the man,
If any here that loves him, and I afke,
What kindfhip, lenitie, or chriftian raigne,
Rules in the man, to barre this foule impeach ?
Firft I inferre the *Chefters* banifhment :
For reprehending him in moft unchriftian crimes,
Was fpeciall notice of a tyrants will.
But were this all, the divell fhould be fav'd,
But this the leaft of many thoufand faults,
That circumftance with leifure might difplay.
Our private wrongs, no parcell of my tale
Which now in prefence, but for fome great caufe
Might wifh to him as to a mortall foe.
But fhall I clofe the period with an act
Abhorring in the eares of chriftian men,
His coufins death, that fweet unguiltie child,
Untimely butcherd by the tyrants meanes,
Here are my proofes, as cleere as gravel brooke,
And on the fame I further muft inferre,

That

That who upholds a tyrant in his courfe,
Is culpable of all his damned guilt.
To fhew the which, is yet to be defcrib'd.
My lord of *Pembrooke*, fhewe what is behinde,
Onely I fay, that were there nothing elfe
To moove us, but the popes moft dreadfull curfe,
Whereof we are affured, if we faile,
It were enough to inftigate us all,
With earneftneffe of fprite, to feeke a meane
To difpoffeffe *John* of his regiment.

Pembrooke.

Well hath my lord of *Effex* told his tale,
Which I averre for moft fubftantiall truth,
And more to make the matter to our minde,
I fay that *Lewis* in challenge of his wife,
Hath title of an uncontrouled plea,
To all that longeth to our *Englifh* crowne.
Short tale to make, the fea apoftolike,
Hath offerd difpenfation for the fault.
If any be, as truft me none I know,   .
By planting *Lewis* in the ufurpers roome:
This is the caufe of all our prefence here,
That on the holy altar we proteft,
To aid the right of *Lewis* with goods and life,
Who on our knowledge is in armes for *England.*
What fay you lords?

Salifburie.

As *Pembrooke* faith, affirmeth *Salifburie*:
Faire *Lewis* of *France* that fpoufed lady *Blanch*,
Hath title of an uncontrouled ftrength
To *England*, and what longeth to the crowne:
In right whereof, as we are true inform'd,
The prince is marching hitherward in armes.
Our purpofe, to conclude that with a word,
Is to inveft him as we may devife,
King of our countrey, in the tyrants ftead :
And fo the warrant on the altar fworne,
And fo the intent for which we hither came.

Baftard.

My lord of *Salifburie*, I cannot couch
My fpeeches with the needfull words of arte,

As

As doth befeeme in fuch a waightie worke,
But what my confcience and my duty will,
I purpofe to impart.
For *Cheflers* exile, blame his bufie wit,
That medled where his duty quite forbade :
For any private caufes that you have,
Me thinke they fhould not mount to fuch a height,
As to depofe a king in their revenge.
For *Arthurs* death, K. *John* was innocent,
He defperate was the deathfman to himfelfe,
Which you, to make a colour to your crime, injuftly do im-
        pute to his defalt,
But wher fel traitorifme hath refidence,
There wants no words to fet defpight on worke.
I fay tis fhame, and worthy all reproofe,
To wreft fuch petty wrongs in tearms of right,
Againft a king annointed by the lord.
Why *Salfburie*, admit the wrongs are true,
Yet fubjects may not take in hand revenge,
And rob the heavens of their proper power,
Where fitteth he to whom revenge belongs.
And doth a pope, a prieft, a man of pride,
Give charters for the lives of lawfull kings ?
What can he bleffe, or who regards his curfe,
But fuch as give to man, and take from God ?
I fpeake it in the fight of God above,
There's not a man that dies in your beleefe,
But fels his foule perpetually to paine.
Aid *Lewis*, leave God, kill *John*, pleafe hell,
Make havocke of the welfare of your foules,
For here I leave you in the fight of heaven,
A troope of traytors, food for hellifh fiends ;
If you defift, then follow me as friends,
If not, then doe your worft, as hatefull traytors.
For *Lewis* his right, alaffe tis too too lame,
A fenfleffe claime, if truth be titles friend.
In briefe, if this be caufe of our refort,
Our pilgrimage is to the divels fhrine.
I came not lords, to troupe as traytors doe,
Nor will I counfell in fo bad a caufe :

Pleafe

Pleafe you returne, we goe againe as friends,
If not, I to my king, and you where traytors pleafe. [*Exit.*

Percie.

A hot yong man, and fo my lords proceed,
I let him goe, and better loft than found.

Pembrooke.

What fay you lords, will all the reft proceed,
Will you all with me fweare upon the altar,
That you wil to the death, be aid to *Le.* and enemy to *John?*
Every man lay his hand by mine, in witnes of his harts accord,
Wel then, every man to armes to meet the king,
Who is already before *London.*

Enter Meffenger.

Pembrooke.

What newes herauld?

Meffenger.

The right chriftian prince my mafter, *Lewis* of *France*, is at
hand, coming to vifit your honours, directed hither by the right
honourable *Richard* earle of *Bigot*, to conferre with your
honours.

Pembrooke.

How neere is his highneffe?

Meffenger.

Ready to enter your prefence.

Enter Lewis, *earle* Bigot, *with his troupe.*

Lewis.

Faire lords of *England*, *Lewis* falutes you all
As friends, and firme wel-willers of his weale
At whofe requeft, from plentie flowing *France*,
Croffing the ocean with a foutherne gale,
He is in perfon come at your commands,
To undertake and gratifie withall,
The fulneffe of your favours profferd him.
But worlds brave men, omitting promifes,
Till time be minifter of more amends,
I muft acquaint you with our fortunes courfe.
The heavens dewing favours on my head,
Have in their conduct fafe with victory,
Brought me along your well manured bounds,

With

With fmall repulfe, and little croffe of chance.
Your citie *Rochefter*, with great applaufe,
By fome divine inftinct laid armes afide:
And from the hollow holes of *Thamefis*,
Eccho apace repli'd, *Vive le Roy*.
From thence, along the wanton rowling glade
To *Troynouant*, your faire metropolis,
With lucke came *Lewis*, to fhew his troupes of *France*,
Waving our enfignes with the dallying winds,
The fearefull object of fell frowning warre ;
Where after fome affault, and fmall defence,
Heavens may I fay, and not my warlike troupe,
Temperd their hearts to take a friendly foe
Within the compaffe of their high built wals,
Giving me title, as it feemd they wifh.
Thus fortune (lords) acts to your forwardneffe,
Meanes of content, in lieu of former griefe :
And may I live but to requite you all,
Worlds wifh were mine, in dying noted yours.

                Salifbury.
Welcom the balme that clofeth up our wounds,
The foveraigne medcine for our quicke recure,
The anchor of our hope, the onely prop,
Whereon depends our lives, our lands, our weale,
Without the which, as fheepe without their heird,
(Except a fhepheard winking at the wolfe)
We ftray, we pine, we run to thoufand harmes.
No marvell then, though with unwonted joy,
We welcome him that beateth woes away.

                Lewis.
Thanks to you all of this religious league,
A holy knot of catholike confent.
I cannot name you lordings, man by man,
But like a ftranger unacquainted yet,
In generall I promife faithfull love :
Lord *Bigot* brought me to S. *Edmunds* fhrine,
Giving me warrant of a chriftian oath,
That this affembly came devoted here,
To fweare according as your packets fhow'd,
Homage and loyall fervice to our felfe,

        T 4

                              I need

I need not doubt the furetie of your wils,
Since well I know, for many of your fakes,
The townes have yeelded on their own accords:
Yet for a fashion, not for misbeleefe,
My eyes muft witneffe, and thefe eares muft heare
Your oath upon the holy altar fworne,
And after march, to end our commings caufe.

Salfbury.

That we intend no other than good truth,
All that are prefent of this holy league,
For confirmation of our better truft,
In prefence of his highneffe, fweare with me,
The fequel that myfelfe fhall utter here.

I *Thomas Plantaginet*, earle of *Salifburie*, fweare upon the altar, and by the holy army of faints, homage and allegeance to the right chriftian prince *Lewis* of *France*, as true and right-full king to *England*, *Cornewall*, and *Wales*, and to their terri-tories: in the defence whereof, I upon the holy altar fweare all forwardneffe.   [*All the* Eng. Lo. *fweare.*

As the noble earle hath fworne, fo fweare we all.

Lewis.

I reft affured on your holy oath,
And on this altar in like fort I fweare
Love to you all, and princely recompence
To guerdon your good wils unto the full.
And fince I am at this religious fhrine,
My good wel-willers give us leave a while,
To ufe fome orizons our felves apart,
To all the holy company of heaven,
That they will fmile upon our purpofes,
And bring them to a fortunate event.

Salfbury.

We leave your highneffe to your good intent.
[*Exeunt lords of* Englar.

Lewis.

Now vicount *Meloun*, what remains behind?
Truft me thefe traytors to their foveraigne ftate,
Are not to be beleev'd in any fort.

Meloun.

Indeed my lord, they that infringe their oths,
And play the rebels gainft their native king,

Will

Will for as little caufe revolt from you,
If ever opportunitie incite them fo:
For once forfworne, and never after found,
There's no affiance after perjury.

Lewis.

Well *Meloun*, wel, let's fmooth with them awhile,
Untill we have as much as they can doe:
And when their vertue is exhaled drie,
Ile hang them for the guerdon of their helpe:
Meane while wee'l ufe them as a pretious poyfon,
To undertake the iffue of our hope.

Fr. Lord.

Tis policy (my lord) to baite our hookes
With merry fmiles, and promife of much weight:
But when your highneffe needeth them no more,
'Tis good make fure worke with them, left indeede
They proove to you as to their naturall king.

Meloun.

Truft mee my lord, right well have you advifde,
Venome for ufe, but never for a fport
Is to be dallied with, left it infect.
Were you inftald, as foone I hope you fhall:
Be free from traitors, and difpatch them all.

Lewis.

That fo I meane, I fweare before you all
On this fame altar, and by heavens power,
Theres not an *Englifh* traitor of them all,
John once difpatcht, and I faire *Englands* king,
Shall on his fhoulders beare his head one day,
But I will crop it for their guilts defert:
Nor fhall their heires injoy their feigniories,
But perifh by their parents foule amiffe.
This have I fworne, and this will I performe,
If ere I come unto the height I hope.
Lay downe your hands, and fweare the fame with me.

[*The* French *lords fweare.*

Why fo, now call them in, and fpeake them faire,
A fmile of *Fraunce* will feed an *Englifh* foole.
Beare them in hand as friends, for fo they be:
But in the heart like traitors as they are.

Enter

Enter the English *lords.*

Now famous followers, chiefetaines of the world,
Have we follicited with hearty prayer
The heaven in favour of our high attempt.
Leave we this place, and march we with our power
To rowfe the tyrant from his chiefeft hold :
And when our labours have a profprous end,
Each man fhall reape the fruit of his defert.
And fo refolv'd, brave followers let us hence.

Enter K. John, Baftard, Pandulph, *and a many priefts with them.*

Pandulph.
Thus *John,* thou art abfolv'd from all thy finnes,
And freed by order from our fathers curfe.
Receive thy crowne againe, with this provifo,
That thou remaine true liegeman to the pope,
And carry armes in right of holy *Rome.*
John.
I holde the fame as tenant to the pope,
And thanke your holineffe for your kindneffe fhewne.
Philip.
A proper jeft, when kings muft ftoop to friers,
Need hath no law, when friers muft be kings.

Enter a Meffenger.

Meffenger.
Pleafe it your majeftie, the prince of *France,*
With all the nobles of your graces land
Are marching hitherward in good aray.
Where ere they fet their foot, all places yeeld :
Thy land is theirs, and not a foot holds out
But *Dover* caftle, which is hard befieg'd.
Pandulph.
Feare not king *John,* thy kingdome is the popes,
And they fhall know his holineffe hath power,
To beate them foone from whence he hath to doe.

Drum.

Drums and trumpets. *Enter* Lewes, Melun, Salisbury, Essex,
Pembrooke, *and all the nobles from* Fraunce *and* England.

Lewes.

Pandulph, as gave his holinesse in charge,
So hath the *Dolphin* mustred up his troupes,
And wonne the greatest part of all this land.
But ill becomes your grace lord Cardinall,
Thus to converse with *John* that is accurst.

Pandulph.

Lewes of *France,* victorious conqueror,
Whose sword hath made this iland quake for feare;
Thy forwardnesse to fight for holy *Rome,*
Shall be remunerated to the full:
But know my lord, K. *John* is now absolv'd,
The Pope is pleasde, the land is blest agen,
And thou hast brought each thing to good effect.
It resteth then that thou withdraw thy powers,
And quietly returne to *Fraunce* againe:
For all is done the pope would wish thee doe.

Lewes.

But all's not done that *Lewes* came to do.
Why *Pandulph,* hath king *Philip* sent his sonne
And beene at such excessive charge in warres,
To be dismist with words? king *John* shall know,
England is mine, and he usurps my right.

Pandulph.

Lewes, I charge thee and thy complices
Upon the paine of *Pandulphs* holy curse,
That thou withdraw thy powers to *Fraunce* againe,
And yeeld up *London* and the neighbour townes
That thou hast tane in *England* by the sword.

Melun.

Lord Cardinall by *Lewes* princely leave,
It can be nought but usurpation
In thee, the pope, and all the church of *Rome,*
Thus to insult on kings of *Christendome,*
Now with a word to make them carrie armes,
Then with a word to make them leave their armes.
This must not be: prince *Lewes* keepe thine owne,
Let pope and popelings curse their bellies full.

Bastard.

Baſtard.

My lord of *Melun*, what title had the prince
To *England* and the crowne of *Albion*,
But ſuch a title as the pope confirm'd :
The prelate now lets fall his fained claime :
Lewes is but the agent for the pope,
Then muſt the *Dolphin* ceaſe, ſith he hath ceaſt :
But ceaſe or no, it greatly matters not,
If you my lords and barons of the land
Will leave the *French*, and cleave unto our king.
For ſhame yee peeres of *England* ſuffer not
Your ſelves, your honours, and your land to fall :
But with reſolved thoughts beate backe the *French*,
And free the land from yoke of ſervitude.

Saliſbury.

Philip, not ſo, lord *Lewes* is our king,
And wee will follow him unto the death.

Pandulph.

Then in the name of *Innocent* the Pope,
I curſe the prince and all that take his part,
And excommunicate the rebell peeres
As traitors to the king and to the pope.

Lewes.

Pandulph, our ſwords ſhall bleſſe our ſelves agen :
Prepare thee *John*, lords follow me your king.   [*Exeunt.*

John.

Accurſed *John*, the divell owes thee ſhame,
Reſiſting *Rome*, or yeelding to the pope, all's one.
The divell take the pope, the peeres, and *Fraunce:*
Shame be my ſhare for yeelding to the prieſt.

Pandulph.

Comfort thy ſelfe king *John*, the cardnall goes
Upon his curſe to make them leave their armes.   [*Exit.*

Baſtard.

Comfort my lord, and curſe the cardinall,
Betake your ſelfe to armes, my troupes are preſt
To anſwer *Lewes* with a luſtie ſhocke :
The *Engliſh* archers have their quivers full,
Their bowes are bent, the pikes are preſt to puſh :
Good cheere my lord, king *Richards* fortune hangs
Upon the plume of warrelike *Philips* helme.

Then

Then let them know his brother and his fonne
Are leaders of the *Englishmen* at armes.
John.
Philip, I know not how to anfwer thee:
But let us hence, to anfwer *Lewes* pride.

Excurfions. *Enter* Meloun *with* Englifh *lords.*
Meloun.
O I am flaine, nobles, *Salisbury, Pembrooke,*
My foule is charged, heare me: for what I fay
Concerns the peeres of *England,* and their ftate.
Liften, brave lords, a fearefull mourning tale
To be delivered by a man of death.
Behold thefe fearres, the dole of bloudie *Mars*
Are harbingers from natures common foe,
Citing this truncke to *Tellus* prifon houfe?
Lifes charter (lordings) lafteth not an houre:
And fearefull thoughts, forerunners of my end,
Bids me give phyficke to a fickely foule.
O peeres of *England,* know you what you do?
There's but a haire that funders you from harme,
The hooke is baited, and the traine is made,
And fimply you runne doating to your deaths.
But left I die, and leave my tale untolde,
With filence flaughtering fo brave a crew,
This I averre, if *Lewes* winne the day,
There's not an *Englifhman* that lifts his hand
Againft king *John* to plant the heire of *France,*
But is already damnd to cruell death.
I heard it vow'd; my felfe amongft the reft
Swore on the altar aide to this edict.
Two caufes lords, makes me difplay this drift,
The greateft for the freedome of my foule,
That longs to leave this manfion free from guilt:
The other on a naturall inftinct,
For that my grandfire was an *Englifhman.*
Mifdoubt not lords the truth of my difcourfe,
No frenfie, nor no brainficke idle fit,
But well advifde, and wotting what I fay,
Pronounce I here before the face of heaven,

That

That nothing is difcovered but a truth.
Tis time to flie, fubmit your felves to *John*,
The fmiles of *Fraunce* fhade in the frownes of death,
Lirt up your fwords, turne face againft the *French*,
Expell the yoke that's framed for your necks.
Backe warremen, backe, imbowell not the clime,
Your feate, your nurfe, your birth dayes breathing place,
That bred you, beares you, brought you up in armes.
Ah! be not fo ingrate to digge your mothers grave,
Preferve your lambes and beate away the wolfe.
My foule hath faid, contritions penitence
Laies hold on mans redemption for my finne.
Farewell my lords; witneffe my faith when we are met in
      heaven,
And for my kindneffe give me grave roome here.
My foule doth fleet, worlds vanities farewell.

                 Salfbury.
   Now joy betide thy foule well-meaning man,
How now my lords, what cooling carde is this?
A greater griefe growes now than earft hath beene.
What counfell give you, fnall we ftay and die?
Or fhall we home, and kneele unto the king.

                 Pembrooke.
   My heart mifgave this fad accurfed newes :
What have we done? fie lords, what frenfie moved
Our hearts to yeeld unto the pride of *Fraunce?*
If we perfever, we are fure to die :
If we defift, fmall hope againe of life.

                 Salfbury.
   Beare hence the body of this wretched man,
That made us wretched with his dying tale,
And ftand not wayling on our prefent harmes,
As women wont : but feeke our harmes redreffe.
As for my felfe, I will in hafte be gone :
And kneele for pardon to our foveraign *John.*

                 Pemboooke.
   I, there's the way, lets rather kneele to him,
Than to the *French* that would confound us all.   [*Exeunt.*

                               Enter

Enter king John *carried betweene two lords.*

John.

Set downe, fet downe the loade not worth your paine,
For done I am with deadly wounding griefe:
Sickely and fuccourleffe, hopeleffe of any good,
The world hath wearied me, and I have wearied it:
It loathes I live, I live and loathe my felfe.
Who pities me? to whom have I beene kinde?
But to a few; a few will pitie me.
Why die I not? death fcornes fo vilde a prey.
Why live I not, life hates fo fad a prize.
I fue to both to be retaind of either,
But both are deafe, I can be heard of neither.
Nor death nor life, yet life and neare the neere,
Ymixt with death, biding I wot not where.

Philip.

How fares my lord, that he is carried thus?
Not all the aukeward fortunes yet befalne,
Made fuch impreffion of lament in me.
Nor ever did my eye attaint my heart
With any object mooving more remorfe,
Than now beholding of a mighty king,
Borne by his lords in fuch diftreffed ftate.

John.

What newes with thee? if bad, report it ftraight:
If good, be mute, it doth but flatter me.

Philip.

Such as it is, and heavy though it be,
To glut the world with tragicke elegies,
Once will I breathe to aggravate the reft,
Another moane to make the meafure full.
The braveft bow-man had not yet fent forth
Two arrowes from the quiver at his fide,
But that a rumor went throughout our campe,
That *John* was fled, the king had left the field.
At laft the rumor fcal'd thefe eares of mine,
Who rather chofe as facrifice for *Mars*,
Than ignominous fcandall by retire.
I cheer'd the troupes, as did the prince of *Troy*
His weary followers againft the *Mermidons*,

Crying

Crying alowd, S. *George*, the day is ours.
But feare had captivated courage quite,
And like the lambe before the greedie wolfe,
Se heartlesse fled our war-men from the field.
Short tale to make, my felfe amongft the reft,
Was faine to flie before the eager foe.
By this time night had fhadowed all the earth.
With fable curtaines of the blackeft hue,
And fenc'd us from the furie of the *French*,
As *Io* from the jealous *Junoes* eie,
When in the morning our troupes did gather head,
Paffing the wafhes with our carriages,
The impartiall tide deadly and inexorable,
Came raging in with billowes threatning death,
And fwallowed up the moft of all our men,
My felfe upon a galloway right free, well pac'd,
Out ftript the flouds that followed wave by wave,
I fo efcap'd to tell this tragicke tale.

John.

Griefe upon griefe, yet none fo great a griefe
To end this life, and thereby rid my griefe.
Was ever any fo infortunate,
The right idea of a curfed man,
As I, poore I, a triumph for defpight,
My fever growes, what ague fhakes me fo?
How farre to *Swinftead*, tell me, do you know?
Prefent unto the abbot word of my repaire.
My ficknefle rages, to tyrannize upon me,
I cannot live unleffe this fever leave me.

Philip.

Good cheere my lord, the abbey is at hand,
Behold my lord, the churchmen come to meet you.

Enter the Abbot and certaine Monkes.

Abbot.

All health and happines to our foveraigne lord the king.

John.

Nor health nor happines hath *John* at all.
Say abbot, am I welcome to thy houfe?

5   *Abbot.*

Abbot.

Such welcome as our abbey can afford,
Your majeſtie ſhall be aſſured of.

Philip.

The king thou ſeeſt is weake and very faint,
What victuals haſt thou to refreſh his grace?

Abbot.

Good ſtore my lord, of that you need not feare,
For *Lincolneſhire*, and theſe our abbey grounds
Were never fatter, nor in better plight.

John.

Philip, thou never needſt to doubt of cates,
Nor king nor lord is ſeated halfe ſo well,
As are the abbeis throughout all the land,
If any plot of ground do paſſe another,
The friers faſten on it ſtrait:
But let us in to taſte of their repaſt,
It goes againſt my heart to feed with them,
Or be beholding to ſuch abbey groomes.   [*Exeunt.*

Manet the Monke.

Monke.

Is this the king that never lov'd a frier?
Is this the man that doth contemne the pope?
Is this the man that rob'd the holy church?
And yet will flie unto a friory?
Is this the king that aymes at abbeis lands?
Is this the man whom all the world abhorres,
And yet will flie unto a friorie?
Accurſt be *Swinſtead* abbey, abbot, friers,
Monkes, nunnes, and clarks, and all that dwells therein,
If wicked *John* eſcape alive away.
Now if that thou wilt looke to merit heaven,
And be canonized for a holy ſaint:
To pleaſe the world with a deſerving worke,
Be thou the man to ſet thy countrey free,
And murder him that ſeekes to murder thee.

U   *Enter*

Enter the Abbot.

Abbot.

Why are not you within to cheere the king?
He now begins to mend, and will to meate.

Monke.

What if I fay to ftrangle him in his fleepe?

Abbot.

What, at thy *Mumpfimus?* away,
And feeke fome meanes for to paftime the king.

Monke.

Ile fet a dudgeon dagger at his heart,
And with a mallet knocke him on the head.

Abbot.

Alas, what meanes this monke to murder me?
Dare lay my life hee'l kill me for my place.

Monke.

Ile poyfon him, and it fhall ne'r be knowne,
And then fhall I be chiefeft of my houfe.

Abbot.

If I were dead indeed he is the next,
But Ile away, for why the monke is mad,
And in his madneffe he will murder me.

Monke.

My L. I cry your lordfhip mercy, I faw you not.

Abbot.

Alas good *Thomas* do not murder me, and thou fhalt have my
place with thoufand thanks.

Monke.

I murder you! God fhield from fuch a thought.

Abbot.

If thou wilt needs, yet let me fay my prayers.

Monke.

I will not hurt your lordfhip good my lord : but if you pleafe,
I will impart a thing that fhall be beneficiall to us all.

Abbot.

Wilt thou not hurt me holy monke? fay on,

Monke.

You know my lord, the king is in our houfe.

Abbot.

True.

5

Monke.

Monke.

You know likewise the king abhorres a frier.

Abbot.

True.

Monke.

And he that loves not a frier is our enemy.

Abbot.

Thou faift true.

Monke.

Then the king is our enemy.

Abbot.

True.

Monke.

Why then fhould we not kil our enemy, and the king being our enemy, why then fhould we not kill the K.

Abbot.

O bleffed monke! I fee God moves thy minde to free this land from tyrants flavery.

But who dare venter for to do this deede?

Monke.

Who dare? why I my lord dare do the deed,

Ile free my country and the church from foes,

And merit heaven by killing of a king.

Abbot.

Thomas kneele downe, and if thou art refolv'd,

I will abfolve thee here from all thy finnes,

For why the deed is meritorious.

Forward, and feare not man, for every month,

Our friers fhall finge a maffe for *Thomas* foule.

Monke.

God and S. *Francis* profper my attempt,

For now my lord I goe about my worke.   [*Exeunt.*

Enter Lewes *and his armie.*

Lewes.

Thus victorie in bloudie lawrell clad,

Followes the fortune of yong *Lodowike*,

The *Englifhmen* as danted at our fight,

Fall as the fowle before the eagles eies,

Onely two croffes of contrary change

U 2   D●

Do nip my heart, and vex me with unreſt.
Lord *Meluns* death, the one part of my ſoule,
A braver man did never live in *Fraunce.*
The other griefe, I that's a gall indeed,
To thinke that *Dover* caſtle ſhould hold out
Gainſt all aſſaults, and reſt impregnable.
Yee warrelike race of *Francus Hectors* ſonne,
Triumph in conqueſt of that tyrant *John,*
The better halfe of *England* is our owne :
And towards the conqueſt of the other part,
We have the face of all the *Engliſh* lords,
What then remaines but overrunne the land ?
Be reſolute my warrelike followers,
And if good fortune ſerve as ſhee begins,
The pooreſt peſant of the realme of *France*
Shal be a maſter ore an *Engliſh* lord.

Enter a meſſenger.

Lewes.

Fellow, what newes ?

Meſſenger.

Pleaſeth your grace, the earle of *Salſbury, Penbrooke, Eſſex,*
Clare, and *Arundell,* with all the barons that did fight for
thee, are on a ſodaine fled with all their powers, to joyne
with *John,* to drive thee backe againe.

Enter another meſſenger.

Meſſenger.

Lewes my lord, why ſtandſt thou in a maze ?
Gather thy troupes, hope not of helpe from *Fraunce,*
For all thy forces being fiftie ſaile,
Containing twenty thouſand ſouldiers,
With victuall and munition for the warre,
Putting them from *Callis* in unluckie time,
Did croſſe the ſeas, and on the *Goodwin* ſands,
The men, munition, and the ſhips are loſt.

Enter another meſſenger.

Lewes.

More newes ? ſay on.

Meſſenger.

Meſſenger.

John (my lord) with all his ſcattered troups,
Flying the fury of your conquering ſword,
As *Pharaoh* earſt within the bloody ſea,
So he and his environed with the tide,
On *Lincolne* waſhes all were overwhelmed,
The barons fled, our forces caſt away.

Lewes.

Was ever heard ſuch unexpected newes?

Meſſenger.

Yet *Lodowike* revive thy dying heart,
King *John* and all his forces are confumde.
The leſſe thou needſt the aid of *Engliſh* earles,
The leſſe thou needſt to grieve thy navies wracke,
And follow times advantage with ſucceſſe.

Lewes.

Brave *Frenchmen* arm'd with magnanimitie,
March after *Lewes*, who will leade you on
To chafe the barons power that wants a head,
For *John* is drown'd, and I am *Englands* king.
Though our munition and our men be loſt,
Philip of *Fraunce* will ſend us freſh ſupplies.　　　　[*Exeunt.*

Enter two friers laying a cloth.

Frier.

Diſpatch, diſpatch, the king deſires to eate,
Would a might eate his laſt for the love he bears to church men.

Frier.

I am of thy mind too, and ſo it ſhould be and we might
be our owne carvers.
I marvell why they dine here in the orchard.

Frier.

I know not, nor I care not. The king comes.

John.

Come on lord *Abbot*, ſhall we ſit together?

Abbot.

Pleaſeth your grace ſit downe.

John.

Take your places ſirs, no pomp in penury, all beggers and
friends may come, where neceſſitie keepes the houſe, curteſie
is barr'd the table, ſit downe *Philip.*

　　　　　　　　　　　Baſtard

Baftard.

My lord, I am loth to allude fo much to the proverb, honors change maners : a king is king, though fortune do her worft, and we as dutifull in defpite of her frowne, as if your highnes were now in the higheft tipe of dignitie.

John.

Come, no more adoe, and you tell mee much of dignity, you'l marre my appetite in a furfet of forrow.
What cheere lord *Abbot*, me thinks ye frown like an hoft that knows his gueft hath no money to pay the reckning ?

Abbot.

No my liege, if I frowne at all, it is for I feare this cheere too homely to entertaine fo mighty a gueft as your majeftie.

Baftard.

I think rather, my lord *Abbot*, you remember my laft being here, when I went in progreffe for powches, and the rancor of his heart breakes out in his countenance, to fhew he hath not forgot me.

Abbot.

Not fo my lord, you, and the meaneft follower of his majefty, are heartily welcome to me.

Monke.

Waffell my liege, and as a poore monke may fay, welcome to *Swinftead.*

John.

Begin monke, and report hereafter thou waft tafter to a king.

Monke.

As much health to your highneffe as mine owne heart.

John.

I pledge thee kind monke.

Monke.

The merrieft draught that ever was drunke in *England.*
Am I not too bold with your highneffe ?

John.

Not a whit, all friends and fellowes for a time.

Monke.

If the inwards of a tod be a compound of any proofe : why fo it workes.

John.

Stay *Philip*, where's the monke ?

Baftard.

Baſtard.

He is dead my lord.

John.

Then drinke not *Philip* for a world of wealth.

Baſtard.

What cheere my liege ? your collor gins to change.

John.

So doth my life : O *Philip*, I am poiſon'd.
The monke, the divell, the poyſon gins to rage,
It will depoſe my ſelfe a king from raigne.

Baſtard.

This abbot hath an intereſt in this act.
At all adventures take thou that from me.
There lie the abbot, abbey, lubber, divell.
March with the monke unto the gates of hell.
How fares my lord ?

John.

Philip, ſome drinke, oh for the frozen *Alpes*,
To tumble on and coole this inward heate,
That rageth as the fornace ſeven-fold hote.
To burne the holy tree in *Babylon*,
Power after power forſake their proper power,
Onely the heart impugnes with faint reſiſt
The fierce invade of him that conquers kings,
Helpe God, O paine ! die *John*, O plague
Inflicted on thee for thy grievous ſinnes.
Philip, a chaire, and by and by a grave,
My legges diſdaine the carriage of a king.

Baſtard.

A good my liege, with patience conquer griefe,
And beare this paine with kingly fortitude.

John.

Me thinkes I ſee a catalogue of ſinne,
Wrote by a fiend in marble characters,
The leaſt enough to looſe my part in heaven.
Me thinkes the divell whiſpers in mine eares,
And tells me, tis in vaine to hope for grace,
I muſt be damn'd for *Arthurs* ſodaine death,
I ſee I ſee a thouſand thouſand men
Come to accuſe me for my wrong on earth,

U 4　　　　　　　　　　　　　And

And there is none fo mercifull a God
That will forgive the number of my finnes.
How have I liv'd, but by anothers loffe?
What have I lov'd, but wracke of others weale?
Where have I vow'd, and not infring'd mine oath?
Where have I done a deede deferving well?
How, what. when, and where. have I beftow'd a day,
That tended not to fome notorious ill?
My life repleate with rage and tyrannie,
Craves little pittie for fo ftrange a death.
Or, who will fay that *John* deceafde too foone?
Who will not fay, he rather liv'd too long?
Difhonour did attaint me in my life,
And fhame attendeth *John* unto his death.
Why did I fcape the fury of the *French*,
And dide not by the temper of their fwords?
Shame.efie my life, and fhamefully it ends,
Scorn'd by my foes, difdained of my friends.

               Baſard.
   Forgive the world and all your earthly foes,
And call on *Chriſt*, who is your lateft friend.

              John.
   My tongue doth falter: *Philip*. I tell thee man,
Since *John* did yeeld unto the prieſt of *Rome*,
Nor he nor his have profpred on the earth:
Curft are his bleffings, and his curfe is bliffe.
But in the fpirit I crie unto my God,
As did the kingly prophet *David* cry,
(Whofe hands, as mine, with murder were attaint)
I am not he fha'l build the lord a houfe,
Or roote thefe locufts from the face of earth:
But if my dying heart deceive me not,
From out thefe loynes fhall fpring a kingly braunch
Whofe armes fhall reach unto the gates of *Rome*,
And with his feete treades downe the ftrumpets pride,
That fits upon the chaire of *Babylon*.
Philip, my heart ftrings breake, the poyfons flame
Hath overcome in me weake natures power,
And in the faith of *Jefu John* doth die.

                            Baſard.

Baſtard.

See how he ſtrives for life, unhappy lord,
Whoſe bowels are divided in themſelves.
This is the fruit of poperie, when true kings
Are ſlaine and ſhouldred out by monkes and friers.

Enter a Meſſenger.

Meſſenger.

Pleaſe it your grace, the barons of the land,
Which all this while bare armes againſt the king,
Conducted by the legate of the Pope,
Together with the prince his highneſſe ſonne,
Do crave to be admitted to the preſence of the king.

Baſtard.

Your ſonne, my lord, young *Henry* craves to ſee
Your majeſtie, and brings with him beſide
The barons that revolted from your grace.
O piercing ſight, he fumbleth in the mouth,
His ſpeech doth faile: lift up your ſelfe my lord,
And ſee the prince to comfort you in death.

Enter Pandulph, *yong* Henry, *the barons with daggers in their
hands.*

Prince.

O let me ſee my father ere he die:
O uncle, were you here, and ſuffred him
To be thus poyſned by a damned monke?
Ah he is dead, father, ſweet father ſpeake.

Baſtard.

His ſpeach doth faile, he haſteth to his end.

Pandulph.

Lords, give me leave to joy the dying king,
With ſight of theſe his nobles kneeling here
With daggers in their hands, who offer up
Their lives for ranſome of their foule offence.
Then good my lord, if you forgive them all,
Lift up your hand in token you forgive.

Saliſbury.

We humbly thanke your royall majeſtie,
And vow to fight for *England* and her king:

And

And in the fight of *John* our foveraigne lord,
In fpite of *Lewes* and the power of *Fraunce*,
Who hitherward are marching in all hafte,
We crowne yong *Henry* in his fathers fted.
Henry.
Help, help, he dies; ah father! looke on mee.
Legate.
K. *John*, farewell: in token of thy faith,
And figne thou dieft the fervant of the lord,
Lift up thy band, that we may witneffe here,
Thou diedft the fervant of our faviour Chrift.
Now joy betide thy foule: what noife is this?

Enter a Meffenger.

Meffenger.
Help lords, the *Dolphin* maketh hitherward
With enfignes of defiance in the winde,
And all our armie ftandeth at a gaze,
Expecting what their leaders will commaund.
Baftard.
Let's arme our felves in yong K. *Henries* right,
And beate the power of *Fraunce* to fea againe.
Legate.
Philip not fo, but I will to the prince,
And bring him face to face to parley with you.
Baftard.
Lord *Salfbury*, your felfe fhall march with me,
So fhall we bring thefe troubles to an end.
King.
Sweet uncle, if thou love thy foveraigne,
Let not a ftone of *Swinftead* abbey ftand,
But pull the houfe about the friers eares:
For they have kill'd my father and my king.   [*Exeunt.*

A parley founded, Lewes, Pandulph, Salifbury, &c.

Pandulph.
Lewes of *Fraunce*, yong *Henry Englands* king
Requires to know the reafon of the claime

That

That thou canſt make to any thing of his.
King *Johu* that did offend, is dead and gone,
See where his breathleſſe trunke in preſence lies,
And he as heire apparant to the crowne
Is now ſucceeded in his fathers roome.

Henry.

Lewes, what law of armes doth leade thee thus,
To keepe poſſeſſion of my lawfull right ?
Anſwere ; in fine, if thou wilt take a peace,
And make ſurrender of my right againe,
Or trie thy title with the dint of ſword :
I tell thee *Dolphin*, *Henry* feares thee not,
For now the barons cleave unto their king,
And what thou haſt in *England* they did get.

Lewes.

Henry of *England*, now that *John* is dead,
That was the chiefeſt enemie to *Fraunce*,
I may the rather be induced to peace.
But *Salſbury*, and you barons of the realme,
This ſtrange revolt agrees not with the oath
That you on *Bury* altare lately ſware.

Salſbury.

Nor did the oath your highneſſe there did take
Agree with honour of the prince of *Fraunce*.

Baſtard.

My lord, what anſwer make you to the king ?

Dolphin.

Faith *Philip* this I ſay : it bootes not me,
Nor any prince, nor power of *Chriſtendome*,
To ſeeke to win this iland *Albion*,
Unleſſe he have a partie in the realme
By treaſon for to help him in his warres.
The peeres which were the partie on my ſide,
Are fled from me : then bootes not me to fight,
But on conditions, as mine honour wills,
I am contented to depart the realme.

Henry.

On what conditions will your highnes yeeld ?

Lewes.

That ſhall we thinke upon by more advice.

Baſtard.

Baftard.

Then kings and princes, let thefe broils have end,
And at more leifure talke upon the league.
Meane while to *Worfter* let us beare the king,
And there interre his bodie, as befeemes.
But firft, in fight of *Lewes* heire or *Fraunce*,
Lords take the crowne, and fet it on his head,
That by fucceffion is our lawfull king.

They crowne yong Henry.

Thus *Englands* peace begins in *Henries* raigne,
And bloodie warres are clofed with happie league.
Let *England* live but true within it felfe,
And all the world can never wrong her ftate.
Lewes, thou fhalt be bravely fhipt to *Fraunce*,
For never *Frenchman* got of *Englifh* ground
The twentith part that thou haft conquered.
Dolphin, thy hand; to *Worfter* we will march:
Lords all, lay hands to beare your foveraigne
With obfequies of honour to his grave:
If *Englands* peeres and people joyne in one,
Nor pope, nor *France*, nor *Spaine* can do them wrong.

F I N I S.

THE

THE

FAMOUS VICTORIES

OF

HENRY ꞏthe FIFTH.

CONTAINING

The Honourable Battell of AGIN-COURT.

As it was acted by the Kinges Majesties Servants.

L O N D O N,

Imprinted by *Barnard Alfop*, and are to be fold by *Tymothie Barlow*, at his fhop in Paules Church-yard, at the Signe of the Bull-head.

THE

FAMOUS VICTORIES

OF

HENRY the FIFTH.

CONTAINING

The Honourable Battell of AGIN-COURT.

Enter the young Prince, Ned, *and* Tom.

Henry the Fifth.

COME away *Ned* and *Tom*.

Both.

Here my lord.

Henry 5.

Come away my lads.
Tell me firs, how much gold have you got.

Ned.

Faith my lord, I have got five hundred pound.

Henry 5.

But tell me *Tom*, how much haſt thou got?

Tom.

Faith my lord, ſome foure hundred pound.

Henry 5.

Foure hundred pounds, bravely ſpoken lads.
But tell me firs, thinke you not that it was a vaillainous part of
me to rob my fathers receyvers?

Ned.

Ned.

Why, no my lord, it was but a tricke of youth.

Henry 5.

Faith *Ned*, thou fayeſt true.'
But tell me ſirs, where abouts are we? ,

Tom.

My lord, we are now about a mile off London.

Henry 5.

But ſirs, I marvell that Sir *John Oldcaſtle*
Comes not away : ſounds ſee where he comes.

Enters Jockey.

How now *Jockey*, what newes with thee ?

Jockey.

Faith my lord, ſuch newes as paſſeth,
For the towne of *Detfort* is riſen,
With hue and crie after your man,
Which parted from us the laſt night,
And has ſet upon, and hath robd a poore carrier.

Henry 5.

Sownes, the villaine that was wont to ſpie
Out our booties.

Jockey.

I my lord, even the very ſame.

Henry 5.

Now baſe-minded raſcall to rob a poore carrier,
Well it ſkils not, ile ſave the baſe villaines life :
I, I may: but tell me *Jockey*, whereabout be the receyvers.

Jockey.

Faith my lord, they are hard by,
But the beſt is, we are a horſe backe, and they be a foote,
So we may eſcape them.

Henry 5.

Well, I the villaines come, let mee alone with them.
But tell me *Jockey*, how much gots thou from the knaves,
For I am ſure I got ſomething, for one of the villaines
So belamde me about the ſhoulders,
As I ſhall feele it this moneth.

Jockey.

Faith my lord, I have got a hundred pound.

3   *Henry.*

Henry 5.

A hundred pound, now bravely fpoken *Jockey*:
But come firs, lay all your money before me,
Now by heaven here is a brave fhew:
But as I am true gentleman, I will have the halfe
Of this fpent to night, but firs, take up your bags.
Here comes the Receyvers, let me alone.

Enters two Receyvers.

One.

Alas good fellow, what fhall we doe?
I dare never go home to the court, for I fhall be hangde,
But here is the yong Prince, what fhall we do?

Henry 5.

How now you villaines, what are you?

One Receyver.

Speake you to him.

Other.

No I pray, fpeake you to him.

Henry.

Why how now you rafcals, why fpeake you not?

One.

Forfooth we be, pray fpeake you to him.

Henry 5.

Sowns, villaines fpeake, or ile cut off your heads.

Other.

Forfooth he can tell the tale better then I.

One.

Forfooth we be your fathers Receyvers.

Henry 5.

Are you my fathers Receyvers.
Then I hope yee have brought me fome money.

One.

Money: alaffe fir wee be robd.

Henry 5.

Robd, how many were there of them?

One.

Marry fir there were foure of them,
And one of them had Sir *John Oldcaftles* bay Hobbey,
And your blacke nag.

X   *Henry*

Henry 5.

Gogs wounds how like you this *Jockey*,
Blood you villaines : my father robd of his money abroad,
And we in our ftables.
But tell me how many were there of them.

One Receyver.

If it pleafe you, there were foure of them,
And there was one about the bigneffe of you :
But I am fure I fo belamde him about the fhoulders,
That he will feele it this moneth.

Henry 5.

Gogs wounds you lambde them fairely,
So that they have carryed away your money.
But come firs what fhall we doe with the villaines.

Both Receyvers.

I befeech your grace be good to us.

Ned.

I pray you my Lord forgive them this once.
Well ftand up and get you gone,
And looke that you fpeake not a word of it,
For if there be, fownes ile hang you and all your kin.

[*Exit Purfevant.*

Henry 5.

Now firs, how like you this ;
Was not this bravely done :
For now the villaines dare not fpeake a word of it,
I have fo feared them with words.
Now whether fhall we go.

All.

Why my lord, you know our old Hofteffe at *Feverfham.*

Henry 5.

Our Hofteffe at *Feverfham,* bloud what fhall we doe there,   we
have a thoufand pound about us.
And we fhall go to a petty Alehoufe.
No, no : you know the old Taverne in Eaftcheape,
There is good wine : befides there is a pretty wench
That can talke well, for I delight as much in their tongues,
As any part about them.

All.

We are ready to wayte upon your grace.

Henry

Henry 5.

Gogs wounds wait, we will go altogether,
We are all fellowes, I tell you firs, and the King my father
were dead, wee would be all Kings,
Therefore come away.

Ned.

Gogs wounds, bravely fpoken *Harry.*

Enter John Cobler, Robin Pewterer, Lawrence Coftermonger.

John Cobler.

All is well here, all is well Maiters.

Robin.

How fay you, neighbour *John Cobler?*
I think it beft that my neighbour
Robin Pewterer went to Pudding-lane end,
And we will watch here at Billinfgate ward.
How fay you neighbour *Robin,* how like you this?

Robin.

Marry well neighbours:
I care not much if I go to Pudding-lane end.
But neighbours, and you heare any adoe about me,
Make hafte: and if I heare any adoe about you,
I will come to you.   [*Exit* Robin.

Lawrence.

Neighbor what news heare you of the yong Prince?

John.

Marry neighbour, I heare fay, he is a toward young Prince,
For if he meet any by the high way,
He will not let to talke with him,
I dare not call him theefe, but fure he is one of thefe taking
        fellowes.

Lawrence.

Indeed neighbour, I heare fay hee is as lively
A young Prince as ever was.

John.

I, and I heare fay, if he ufe it long,
His father will cut him off from the crowne:
But neighbour fay nothing of that.

Lawrence.

No, no, neighbour I warrant you.

X 2   *John.*

John.

Neighbour, me thinkes you begin to sleepe,
If you will, we will sit downe,
Fot I thinke it is about midnight.

Lawrence.

Marry content neighbour, let us sleepe.

Enter Dericke *roving.*

Dericke.

Who, who there, who there ?   [*Exit* Dericke.

Enter Robin.

Robin.

O neighbours, what meane you to sleepe,
And such adoe in the streetes ?

Ambo.

How now neighbour, whats the matter ?

Enter Dericke *againe.*

Dericke.

Who there, who there, who there ?

Cobler.

Why, what ayleft thou ? here is no horses.

Dericke.

O alas man, I am robd, who there, who there ?

Robin.

Hold him neighbour *Cobler.*

Cobler.

Why I fee thou art a plaine clowne.

Dericke.

Am I a clowne, fownes mafters,
Do clownes goe in filke apparrel.
I am fure all we gentlemen clownes in *Kent* fcant goe fo well :
Sounes you know clownes very well.
Heare you, are you Mafter Conftable, and you be fpeake ;
For I will not take it at his hands.

John.

Faith I am not Mafter Conftable,
But I am one of his bad officers, for he is not here.

[*Dericke.*

Dericke.

Is not mafter Conftable here?
Well it is no matter, Ile have the law at his hands.

John.

Nay I pray you do not take the law of us.

Dericke.

You are one of his beaftly officers.

John.

I am one of his bad officers.

Dericke.

Why then I charge thee looke to him.

Cobler.

Nay but heare yee fir, you feeme to be an honeft
Fellow, and we are poore men, and now tis night,
And we would be loath to have any thing adoo,
Therefore I pray thee put it up.

Dericke,

Firft, thou fayeft true, I am an honeft fellow,
And a proper handfome fellow too,
And you feem to be poore men, therfore I care not greatly,
Nay I am quickly pacified,
But and you chance to fpie the theefe,
I pray you lay hold on him.

Robin.

Yes that we will, I warrant you.

Dericke.

Tis a wonderfull thing to fee how glad the knave is, now I
have forgiven him.

John.

Neighbours, doe yee looke about you,
How now, who's there?

Enter the theefe.

Theefe.

Here is a good fellow, I pray you which is the way to the
olde Taverne in Eaftcheape.

Dericke,

Whoope hollo, now *Gadshill*, knoweft thou mee?

Theefe.

I know thee for an affe.

Derick.

Dericke.

And I know thee for a taking fellow.
Upon Gads hill in Kent.
A bots light upon you.

Theefe.

The worson villaine would be knockt.

Dericke.

Masters, villaine, and ye be men stand to him,
And take his weapon from him, let him not passe you,

John.

My friend, what make you abroad now?
It is too late to walke now.

Theefe.

It is not too late for true men to walke.

Lawrence.

We know thee not to be a true man.

Theefe.

Why what doe you meane to doe with me?
Sounes I am one of the Kings liege people.

Dericke.

Heare you sir, are you one of the kings liege people?

Theefe.

I marry am *I* sir, what say you to it?

Dericke.

Marry sir, I say you are one of the Kings filching people,

Cobler.

Come, come, lets have him away.

Theefe.

Why what have *I* done.

Robin.

Thou hast robd a poore fe'low,
And taken away his goods from him.

Theefe.

I never saw him before.

Dericke.

Maisters who comes here?

Enter the Vintners boy.

Boy.

How now good man Cobler?

Cobler.

Cobler.

How now *Robin*, what makes thou abroade
At this time of night?

Boy.

Marrie I have bene at the Counter,
I can tell fuch newes as never you have hearde the like.

Cobler.

What is that *Robin*, what is the matter?

Boy.

Why this night about two houres agoe, there came the
young Prince, and three or foure more of his companions,
and called for wine good ftore, and then they fent for a noyfe
of mufitians, and were very merry for the fpace of an houre,
then whether their muficke liked them not, or whether they
had drunke too much wine or no, I cannot tell, but our pots
flew againft the walls, and then they drewe their fwords, and
went into the ftreet and fought, and fome tooke one part, and
fome tooke another, but for the fpace of halfe an houre,
there was fuch a bloody fray as paffeth, and none could parte
them untill fuch time as the Mayor and Sheriffe were fent for,
and then at laft, with much adoo, they tooke them, and fo the
young Prince was carryed to the Counter, and then about
one houre after, there came a meffenger from the court in all
hafte, from the King, for my Lorde Mayor and the Sheriffe,
but for what caufe I know not.

Cobler.

Here is newes indeed *Robert.*

Lawrence.

Marry Neighbour, this newes is ftrange indeede, I thinke it
beft Neighbour, to rid our hands of this fellow firft.

Theefe.

What meane you to doo with me?

Cobler.

Wee meane to carry you to the prifon, and there to remaine till the feffions day.

Theefe.

Then I pray you let me go to the prifon where my maifter is.

Cobler.

Nay. thou muft goe to the countrey prifon, to Newgate,
therefore come away.

X 4　　　　　　　　　　　*Theefe.*

Theefe.

I prethee be good to me honeſt fellow.

Dericke.

I marry will I, ile be very charitable to thee,
For I wil never leave thee, til I ſee thee on the gallows.

Enter **Henry** *the fourth, with the Earle of* **Exeter,** *and the Lord of* **Oxford.**

Oxford.

And pleaſe your majeſtie, here is my Loid Mayor, and the
Sheriffe of London, to ſpeake with your majeſtie.

K. Henry 4.

Admit them to our preſence.

Enter the L. Mayor, and the Sheriffe.

King.

Now my good Lord Mayor of London,
The cauſe of my ſending for you at this time, is to tell you
of a matter which I have learned of my councell: herein I
underſtand, that you have committed my ſonne to priſon
without our leave and licenſe. What although he be a rude
youth, and likely to give occaſion, yet you might have con-
ſidered that he is a Prince, and my ſonne, and not to be
halled to priſon by every ſubject.

Mayor.

May it pleaſe your majeſtie to give us leave to tell our tale?

K. Henry 4.

Or elſe God forbid, otheiwiſe you might thinke me an
unequall judge, having more affection to my ſonne, then to
any rightfull judgement.

Mayor.

Then I do not doubt but we ſhal rather deſerve commendations at your majeſties hands, then any anger.

K. Henry 4.

Go to, ſay on.

Mayor.

Then if it pleaſe your majeſtie, this night betwixt two and
three of the clock in the morning my Lord the yong Prince
with a very diſordred company, came to the old Taverne in
Eaſtcheape, and whether it was that their *muſick* liked them
not,

not, or whether they were overcom with wine, I know not, but they drue their fwords, and into the ftreete they went, and fome took my L. the yong Princes part, and fom tooke the other, but betwixt them there was fuch a bloudie fray for the fpace of halfe an houre, that neyther watchmen, nor any other could ftay them, till my brother the Sheriffe of *London* and I were fent for, and at the laft, with much ado we ftayed them, but it was long firft, which was a great difquieting to all your loving fubjects thereabouts : and then my good Lord, we knew not whether your grace had fent them to trie us, whether we would do juftice, or whether it were of their own voluntary will or not, we cannot tell : and therefore in fuch a cafe we knew not what to doe, but for our owne fafegard we fent him to ward, wher he wanteth nothing that is fit for his grace and your majefties fon. And thus moft humbly befeeching your majefty to thinke of our anfwere.

Henry 4.

Stand afide untill we have further deliberated on your anfwere. [*Exit Maior*.

Ah *Harry*, *Harry*, now thrice accurfed *Harry*,
That hath gotten a fonne, which with griefe
Will end his fathers dayes.
O my fonne, a Prince thou art, *I* a Prince in deed,
And to deferve imprifonment,
And well they have done, and like faithfull fubjects:
Difcharge them and let them goe.

L. Exeter.

I befeech your grace be good to my Lorde the young Prince.

Henry 4.

Nay, nay, tis no matter, let him alone.

L. Oxford.

Perchance the Mayor and the Sheriffe have beene too pre-cife in this matter.

Henry 4.

No, they have done like faithfull fubjects,
I will goe my felfe to difcharge them, and let them go.

[*Exeunt omnes*.
Exit
Enter

Enter lord Chiefe Juſtice, Clarke of the Office, Jayler, John
Cobler, Dericke, *and the Theefe.*

Judge.

Jayler bring the priſoner to the barre.

Dericke.

Heare you my Lorde, I pray you bring the barre to the
priſoner.

Judge.

Hold thy hand up at the barre.

Theefe.

Here it is my Lord.

Judge.

Clearke of the office, reade his inditement.

Clearke.

What is thy name?

Theefe.

My name was knowne before I came heere,
And ſhall be when I am gone, I warrant you.

Judge.

I, I thinke ſo, but wee will know it better before thou goe.

Dericke.

Sownes and you doe but ſend to the next Jaile,
We are ſure to know his name ;
For this is not the firſt priſon he hath bene in, ile warrant you.

Clearke.

What is thy name?

Theefe.

What need you to aſke, and have it in writing?

Clearke.

Is not thy name *Cutbert Cutter?*

Theefe.

What the divell neede you aſke, and know it ſo well;

Clearke.

Why then *Cutbert Cutter,* I indite thee by the name of
Cutbert Cutter, for robbing a poore carrier the 20. day of May
laſt paſt, in the fourteen yeare of the raigne of our Soveraigne
Lord King *Henry* the fourth, for ſetting upon a poore carrier
upon Gads hil in Kent, and having beaten and wounded the
ſaid carryer, and taken his goods from him.

Dericke.

Dericke.

Oh maifters ftay there, nay lets never belie the man, for he hath not beaten and wounded me alfo, but he hath beaten and wounded my packe, and hath taken the great race of Ginger, that bouncing *Beff* with the jolly buttocks fhould have had, that grieves me moft.

Judge.

Well, what fayeft thou, art thou guilty, or not guyltie?

Theefe.

Not guilty, my Lord.

Judge.

By whom wilt thou be tride?

Theefe.

By my Lord the young Prince, or by my felfe, whether you will.

Enter the young Prince, with Ned *and* Tom.

Henry 5.

Come away my lads, gogs wounds ye villaine, what make you here? I muft goe about my bufineffe my felfe, and you muft ftand loytering here.

Theefe.

Why my Lord, they have bound mee, and will not let me go.

Henry 5.

Have they bound thee villain, why how now my Lord.

Judge.

I am glad to fee your Grace in good health.

Henry 5.

Why my Lord, this is my man,
Tis marvell you knew him not long before this,
I tell you he is a man of his hands.

Theefe.

I gogs wounds that I am, try me who dare.

Judge.

Your Grace fhall finde fmall credite by acknowledging him to be your man.

Henry 5.

Why my Lord, what hath he done.

Judge.

And it pleafe your majefty, he hath robbed a poore Carrier.

Dericke.

Dericke.

Heare you fir, marry it was one *Dericke*,
Goodman *Hoblings* man of *Kent*.

Henry 5.

What, waft you button breech?
Of my word my Lord, he did it but in jeft.

Judge.

Heare you fir, is it your mans quality to rob folkes in jeft?
In faith he fhall be hangde in earneft.

Henry 5.

Well my Lord, what doe you meane to do with my man?

Judge.

And pleafe your Grace the law muft paffe on him, according to juftice, then he muft be executed.

Dericke.

Heare you fir, I pray you, is it your mans quality to rob
folkes in jeft? In faith he fhall be hangd in jeft.

Henry 5.

Well my Lord once againe, what meane you to doe with
him?

Judge.

And pleafe your Grace according to law and juftice he muft
be hangd.

Henry 5.

Why then belike you meane to hang my man.

Judge.

I am forry that it fals out fo.

Henry 5.

Why my Lord, I pray yee who am I?

Judge.

And pleafe your Grace, you are my L. the yong Prince,
our King that fhall be after the deceafe of our foveraigne
Lord, K. *Henry* the fourth, whom God grant long to raigne.

Henry 5.

You fay true my Lord:
And you will hang my man.

Judge.

And like your Grace, I muft needs doe juftice.

Henry 5.

Tell me my Lord, fhall I have my man?

Judge.

Judge.
I cannot my Lord.

Henry 5.
But will you not let him goe ?

Judge.
I am forry that his cafe is fo ill.

Henry 5.
Tufh, cafe me no cafings, that I have my man ?

Judge.
I cannot, nor I may not my Lord.

Henry 5.
Nay, and I fhall not fay, and then I am anfwered.

Judge.
No.

Henry 5.
No, then I will have him.

He giveth him a boxe on the eare.

Ned.
Gogs wounds my Lord, fhal I cut off his head?

Henry 5.
No, I charge you draw not your fwords,
But get you hence, provide a noyfe of Mufitians,
Away, be gone.   [*Exeunt the Theefe.*

Judge.
Well my Lord, I am content to take it at your hands.

Henry 5.
Nay and you be not, you fhall have more.

Judge.
Why I pray you my Lord, who am I ?

Henry 5.
You, who knowes not you,
Why man, you are Lord chiefe Juftice of England.

Judge.
Your Grace hath faid truth, therfore in ftriking me in this
place, you greatly abufe me, and not me only but alfo your
father: whofe lively perfon here in this place I do reprefent.
And therefore to teach you what prerogatives meane, I commit you to the Fleet, untill wee have fpoken with your father.

Henry

Henry 5.

Why then belike you meane to send mee to the Fleete.

Judge.

I indeed, and therefore carry him away.

[*Exeunt* Henry 5. *with the Officers.*

Judge.

Jayler carry the prisoner to Newgate againe untill the next
Sises.

Jayler.

At your commandement my Lord it shall bee done.

Enter Dericke *and* John Cobler.

Dericke.

Sownds maisters, heres adoo,
When Princes must go to prison:
Why *John*, didst ever see the like?

John.

O *Dericke*, trust me, I never saw the like.

Dericke.

Why *John* thou maist see what princes be in choller,
A Judge a boxe on the eare, Ile tell thee *John*, O *John*,
I would not have done it for twenty shillings.

John.

No nor I, there had beene no way but one with us.
.We should have been hangde.

Dericke.

Faith *John*, Ile tell thee what, thou shalt bee my
Lord chiefe Justice, and thou shalt sit in the chaire,
And ile be the yong Prince, and hit thee a box on the ear
And then thou shalt say, to teach you what prerogatives
meane, I commit you to the Fleete.

John.

Come on, ile be your judge,
But thou shalt not hit me hard.

Dericke.

No, no.

John.

What hath he done?

Dericke.

Marry he hath robd *Dericke*.

4   *John.*

John.

Why then I cannot let him goe.

Dericke.

I muſt needes have my man.

John.

You ſhall not have him.

Dericke.

Shall I not have my man, ſay no and you dare:
How ſay you, ſhall I not have my man ?

John.

No marry ſhall you not.

Dericke.

Shall I not *John* ?

John.

No *Dericke.*

Dericke.

Why then take you that til more come,
Sownes, ſhall I not have him ?

John.

Well I am content to take this at your hand,
But I pray you, who am I ?

Dericke.

Who art thou, fownds, doſt not know thy ſelfe ?

John.

No.

Dericke.

Now away ſimple fellow,
Why man, thou art *John* the Cobler.

John.

No, I am my Lord chiefe Juſtice of England.

Dericke.

Oh *John*, Maſſe thou ſayſt true, thou art indeed.

John.

Why then to teach you what prerogatives mean I commit you to the Fleete.

Dericke.

Wel, I will go, but yfaith you gray beard knave, Ile courſe
you.   [*Exit. And ſtraight enters againe.*
Oh *John*, Com, come out of thy chair, why what a clown
weart thou, to let me hit thee a boxe on the eare, and now
thou

thou feeſt they will not take mee to the Fleet, I thinke that
thou art one of theſe worenday clownes.

John.

But I marvell what will become of thee?

Dericke.

Faith, ile be no more a carrier.

John.

What wilt thou then do?

Dericke.

Iie dweil with thee and be a Cobler.

John.

With me, alaſſe, I am not able to keepe thee,
Why thou wilt eate me out of dores.

Dericke.

Oh *John*, no *John*, I am none of theſe great ſlouching
fellows that devoure theſe great peeces of beefe and brewes,
alaſſe a trifle ſerves me, a woodcocke, a chicken, or a ca-
pons leg, or any ſuch little thing ſerves me.

John.

A capon, why man I cannot get a capon once a yeare,
except it be at Chriſtmas, at ſome other mans houſe, for we
cobiers be glad of a diſh of rootes.

Dericke.

Rootes, why are you ſo good at rooting?
Nay Cobler, weele have you ringde.

John.

But *Dericke* though we be ſo poore,
Yet will we have in ſtore a crab in the fire,
With Nut-browne ale, that is full ſtale,
Which will a man quaile, and lay in the myre.

Dericke.

A hots on you, and be but for your ale,
Ile dwell with you, come lets away as faſt as we can.

[*Exeunt.*

Enter the young Prince with Ned *and* Tom.

Henry 5.

Come away firs, Gogs wounds *Ned*,
Didſt thou not ſee what a boxe on the eare
I tooke my Lord chiefe Juſtice?

Tom.

3

Tom.

By gogs blood it did me good to fee it,
It made his teeth jarre in his head.

Enter Sir John Old-Caftle.

Henry 5.

How now fir *John Old-Caftle* ?
What newes with you ?

John Old-Caftle.

I am glad to fee your Grace at libertie,
I was come I, to vifite you in Prifon.

Henry 5.

To vifite mee, didft thou not know that I am a Princes
fonne ? why tis enough for me to looke into a prifon, thogh
I come not in my felfe, but heres fuch adoo now a dayes,
heres prifoning, heres hanging, whipping, and the divell and
all : but I tell you firs, when I am King, wee will have no
fuch things, but my lads, if the olde King my father were
dead, we would be all Kings.

John Old-Caftle.

He is a good olde man, God take him to his mercie the
fooner.

Henry 5.

But *Ned*, fo foone as I am King, the firft thing I will doo,
fhal be to put my Lord chiefe Juftice out of office, and thou
fhalt be my L. chiefe Juftice of England.

Ned.

Shall I be Lord chiefe Juftice ?
By gogs wounds ile be the braveft Lord chiefe Juftice
That ever was in England.

Henry 5.

Then *Ned*, ile turne all thefe prifons into Fence-fchooles,
and I will endue thee with them, with landes to maintaine
them withall, and then I will have about with my Lord chiefe
Juftice, thou fhalt hang none but pick-purfes, and horfe-
ftealers, and fuch bafe minded villaines, but that fellow that
will ftand by the high-way fide couragioufly, with his fword
and buckler, and take a purfe, that fellowe give him commendations : befide that, fend him to mee, and I will give

Y
him

him an annuall penſion out of my Exchequer, to maintaine him all the dayes of his life.

John.

Nobly ſpoken *Harry*, wee ſhall never have a merry world till the old King be dead.

Ned.

But whether are yee going now?

Henry 5.

To the court, for I heare ſay, my father lyes verie ſicke.

Tom.

But I doubt he will not die.

Henry 5.

Yet will I goe thither, for the breath ſhall be no ſooner out of his mouth, but I will clap the crowne on my head.

Jockey.

Will you goe to the court with that cloake ſo full of needles?

Henry 5.

Cloake. ilat-hoales, needles, and all was of mine owne deviſing, and therefore I will weare it.

Tom.

I pray you (my Lord,) what my bee the meaning thereof?

Henry 5.

Why man, tis a ſigne that I ſtand uppon thornes, till t' crowne be on my head.

Jockey.

Or that every needle might be a pricke to theyr he s that repine at your doings.

Henry 5.

Thou ſayſt true *Jockey*, but theres ſome will ſay, the young Prince will bee a well-toward young-man, and all this geare, that I had as leeve they would breake my head with a pot, as to ſay any ſuch thing, but wee ſtand prating here too long: I muſt needes ſpeake with my father, therefore come away.

Porter.

What a rapping keepe you at the Kings courte gate?

Henry 5.

Heres one that muſt ſpeake with the King.

Porter.

Porter.

The King is very ficke, and none muft fpeake with him.

Henry 5.

No you rafcall, do you not know me.

Porter.

You are my Lord the young Prince.

Henry.

Then go and tell my father, that I muft and will fpeake with him.

Ned.

Shall I cut off his head.

Henry 5.

No, no, though I would helpe you in other places: yet I have nothing to doo here, what you are in my fathers court.

Ned.

I will write him in my tables, for fo foone as I am made Lord chiefe Juftice, I will put him out of his office.

[*The Trumpet founds.*

Henry 5.

Gogs wounds firs, the King comes,
Lets all ftand afide.

Enter the King with the Lord of Exeter.

Henry 4.

And is it true my Lord, that my fonne is already fent to the Fleet: now truly that man is more fitter to rule the realme then I, for by no meanes could I rule my fon, and he by one word hath caufed him to be ruled. Oh my fonne, my fonne, no fooner out of one prifon, but into an other. I had thought one whiles *I* had lived, to have feene this noble realm of England flourifh by thee my fon, but now *I* fee it goes to ruine and decay.   [*He weepes.*

Enters Lord of Oxford.

Oxford.

Þ d pleafe your grace, here is my Lord your fonne,
That commeth to fpeake with you,
He fayth he muft and will fpeake with you.

Henry 4.

Who my fonne *Harry?*

Y 2   *Oxford.*

Oxford.

I and pleafe your majeftie.

Henry 4.

I know wherefore he commeth,
But looke that none come with him.

Oxford.

A very difordered companie, and fuch as make
Very ill rule in your majefties houfe.

Henry 4.

Well, let him come,
But looke that none come with him.   [*He goeth.*

Oxford.

And pleafe your Grace,
My Lord the King fends for you.

Henry 5.

Come away firs, lets goe all together.

Oxford.

And pleafe your grace none muft goe with you.

Henry 5.

Why, I muft needs have them with me,
Otherwife I can doo my father no countenance,
Therefore come away.

Oxford.

The King your father commaunds
There fhould none come.

Henry 5.

Well firs, then be gone,
And provide me three noyfe of mufitians.   [*Exeunt Knights.*

Enters the Prince with a dagger in his hand.

Henry 4.

Come my fonne, come on a Gods name,   •
I know wherefore thy comming is,
Oh my fonne, my fonne, what caufe hath ever bene, ·
That thou fhouldft forfake mee, and followe this vilde and
Reprobate company, which abufeth youth fo manifeftly :
Oh my fonne, thou knoweft that thefe thy doings
Will end thy fathers dayes.   [*He weeps.*
I fo, fo, my fonne, thou feareft not to approach the prefence
of thy ficke father, in that difguifed fort, I tell thee my fonne,
that

that there is never a needle in thy cloke, but it is a pricke to
my heart, and never an ilat-hole, but it is a hole to my foule:
and wherefore thou bringeft that dagger in thy hand I know
not, but by conjecture.   [*He weepes.*

Henry 5.

My confcience accufeth me, moft foveraigne Lord, and
welbeloved father, to anfwere firft to the laft poynt, That is,
whereas you conjecture that this hand and this dagger fhall
be armde againft your life : no, know my beloved father, far
be the thoughts of your fonne, fonne faide I, an unworthy
fonne for fo good a father : but far be the thoughts of any
fuch pretended mifchiefe : and I moft humbly render it to
your majeflies hand, and live my Lord and foveraigne for
ever : and with your dagger arme fhow like vengeance upon
the body of that your fonne, I was about fay, and dare not,
ah woe is me therefore, that your wilde flave, tis not the
Crowne that I come for, fweete Father, becaufe I am unworthy, and thofe wilde and reprobate companions I abandon,
and utterly abolifh their company for ever. Pardon fweet
father, pardon, the leaft thing and moft defire : and this ruf-
fianly cloake, I here teare from my back, and facrifice it to
the divell, which is mafter of all mifchief : pardon me, fweet
father, pardon me : good my Lord of *Exeter*, fpeake for me :
pardon me, pardon, good father : not a word : ah he will not
fpeake one word : A *Harry*, now thrice unhappy *Harry*. But
what fhall I doe : I will go take mee into fome folitary place,
and there lament my finfull life, and when I have done, I
will lay me downe and die.   [*Exit.*

Henry 4.

Call him againe, call my fonne againe.

Henry 5.

And doth my father call me againe ? Now, *Harry*,
Happy be the time that thy father calleth thee againe.

Henry 4.

Stand up my fonne, and do not thinke thy father
But at the requeft of thee my fonne, I will pardon thee,
And God bleffe thee, and make thee his fervant.

Henry 5.

Thanks good my Lord, and no doubt but this day,
Even this day, I am borne new againe.

Y 3   *Henry*

Henry 4.

Come my fon and Lords, take me by the hands.

[*Excunt omnes.*

Enter Dericke.

Dericke.

Thou art a ftinking whore, and a whorfon ftinking whore,
Doeft think it ile take it at thy hands?

Enter John Cobler *running.*

John.

Dericke, D. D. Hearefta,
DOD, never while thou liveft ufe that,
Why what will my neighbours fay, and thou go away fo?

Dericke.

Shees a narrant whore, and ile have the law on you *John.*

John.

Why what hath fhe done?

Dericke.

Marry marke thou *John*,
I will prove it that I will.

John.

What wilt thou prove?

Dericke.

That fhe cald me in to dinner.
John, marke the tale well *John*, and when I was fet
She brought me a difh of roots, and a peece of barell butter
therein: and fhe is a very knave,
And thou a drab if thou take her part.

John.

Hearefta *Dericke*, is this the matter?
Nay, and it be no worfe, we will go home again,
And all fhail be amended.

Dericke.

Oh *John*, hearefta *John*, is all well?

John.

I, all is well.

Dericke.

Then ile go home before, and breake all the glaffe-
windowes.

I

Enter

Enter the King with his Lords.

Henry 4.

Come my Lords, I fee it boots mee not to take any phy-
fike, for all the Phyfitians in the world cannot cure mee, no
not one. But good my Lords, remember my laft Will and
Teftament concerning my fonne, for truely my Lords, I do
not thinke but he will prove as valiant and victorious a King,
as ever raigned in England.

Both.

Let heaven and earth be witneffe betweene us, if wee accomplifh not thy will to the uttermoft.

Henry 4.

I give you moft unfained thankes, good my Lords,
Draw the curtaines and depart my chamber a while,
And caufe fome muficke to rocke me a fleepe.   *[He fleepeth.*
                                            [Exeunt Lords.

Enter the Prince.

Henry 5.

Ah *Harry*, thrice unhappy, that hath neglect fo long from
vifiting of thy ficke father, I will goe, nay but why doe I
not goe to the chamber of my ficke father, to comfort the
melancholy foule of his body, his foule faid I, heere is his
body, but his foule is, wheras it needs no bodie. Now thrice
accurfed *Harry*, that hath offended thy father fo much, and
could not I crave pardon for all. Oh my dying father curft
be the day wherein I was borne, and accurfed be the houre
wherin I was begotten, but what fhall I doe? if weeping
teares which come too late, may fuffice the negligence neglected to fome, I will weepe day and night untill the foun-
taine be drie with weeping.   *[Exit.*

Enter Lord of Exeter *and* Oxford.

Exeter.

Come eafily my Lord, for waking of the King.

Henry 4.

Now my Lords.

Oxford.

How doth your Grace feele your felfe?

Henry.

Henry 4.

Somewhat better after my fleepe,
But good my Lord take off my crowne,
Remove my chayre a little backe, and fet me right.

Ambo.

And pleafe your grace the crown is taken away.

Henry 4.

The crowne taken away,
Good my Lord of *Oxford*, go fee who hath done this deed :
v No doubt tis fome wilde traytor that hath done it,
To deprive my fonne, they that would doe it now,
Would feeke to fcrape and fcrawle for it after my death.

Enter Lord of Oxford *with the Prince.*

Oxford.

Here and pleafe your Grace,
Is my Lord the yong Prince with the Crowne.

Henry 4.

Why how now my fonne,
I had thought the laft time I had you in fchooling,
I had given you a leffon for all,
And do you now begin againe ?
Why tell me my fonne,
Doeft thou thinke the time fo long,
That thou wouldeft have it before the
Breath be out of my mouth.

Henry 5.

Moft foveraigne Lord, and welbeloved father,
I came into your chamber to comfort the melancholy
Soule of your body, and finding you at that time
Paft all recovery, and dead to my thinking,
God is my witneffe, and what fhould I doo,
x But with weeping teares lament the death of you my father,
And after that, feeing the crowne I tooke it :
And tell me my father, who might better take it then I,
After your death, but feeing you live,
I moft humbly render it into your majefties hands,
And the happieft man alive, that my father live :
And live my Lord and father for ever.

Henry.

Henry.

Stand up my fonne,
Thine anfwere hath founded well in mine eares,
For I muft needs confeffe that I was in a very found fleepe,
And altogether unmindfull of thy comming :
But come neare my fonne,
And let mee put thee in poffeffion whilft I live,
That none deprive thee of it after my death.

Henry 5.

Well may I take it at your majefties hands,
But it fhal never touch my head, fo long as my father lives.

[*He taketh the crowne.*

Henry 4.

God give thee joy my fonne,
God bleffe thee, and make thee his fervant,
And fend thee a profperous raigne.
For God knowes my fonne, how hardly I came by it,
And how hardly I have maintained it.

Henry 5.

Howfoever you came by it, I know not,
And now I have it from you, and from you I wil keepe it :
And he that feekes to take the crown from my head,
Let him looke that his armour be thicker then mine,
Or I will pearce him to the heart,
Where it harder then braffe or bollion.

Henry 4.

Nobly fpoken, and like a King.
Now truft me my Lords, I feare not but my fonne
Will be as warlike and victorious a Prince,
As ever raigned in *England.*

L. Ambo.

His former life fhewes no leffe.

Henry 4.

Well my lords I know not whether it be for fleep,
Or drawing neare of drowfie fummer of death,
But I am very much given to fleepe,
Therefore good my lords and my fonne,
Draw the curtaines, depart my chamber,
And caufe fome muficke to rocke me afleepe.   [*Exeunt omnes.*
                                                [*The King dyeth.*
                                                       Enter

Enter the Theefe.

Theefe.

Ah God, I am now much like to a byrd,
Which hath efcaped out of the cage,   ?
For fo foone as my Lord Chiefe Juftice heard
That the old King was dead, he was glad to let me go,
For feare of my Lord the young Prince :
But here comes fome of his companions,
I will fee and I can get any thing of them,
For olde acquaintance.

Enter Knights raunging.

Tom.

Gogs wounds the King is dead.

Jockey.

Dead, then gogs blood, wee fhall be all kings.

Ned.

Gogs wounds, I fhall be Lord Chiefe Juftice of *England.*

Tom.

Why, how are you broken out of prifon ?

Ned.

Gogs wounds, how the villaine ftinkes ?

Jockey.

Why what will become of thee now ?
Fye upon him, how the rafcall ftinkes.

Theefe.

Marry I will goe and ferve my maifter againe.

Tom.

Gogs blood, doeft think that he will have any fuch
Scabd knave as thou art ? What man he is a king now.

Ned.

Hold thee, heres a couple of Angels for thee,
And get thee gone, for the King will not be long
Before he come this way :
And hereafter I will tell the King of thee.   [*Exit Theefe.*

Jockey.

Oh how it did me good to fee the King
When he was crowned.
Me thought his feate was like the figure of heaven,
And his perfon like unto a God.

                                                        Ned.

Ned.

But who would have thought
That the King would have chang'de his countenance fo?

Jockey.

Did you not fee with what grace
He fent his embaffage into *France*, to tell the *French* king
That *Harry* of *England* hath fent for the crowne,
And *Harry* of *England* will have it.

Tom.

But twas but a little to make the people believe,
That hee was forrie for his fathers death.

              [*The trumpets fownds.*

Ned.

Gogs wounds, the King comes,
Lets all ftand afide.

Enter the King with the Archbifhop and the Lord of Oxford.

Jockey.

How doo you my Lord?

Ned.

How now *Harry*?
Tut my Lord, put away thefe dumpes,
You are a King, and all the Realme is yours:
What man? do you not remember the old fayings,
You know I muft be Lord Chiefe Juftice of *England.*
Truft mee my Lord, me thinks you are very much changed:
And 'tis but with a little forrowing, to make folkes believe
The death of your father grieves you,
And 'tis nothing fo.

Henry 5.

I prethee *Ned* mend thy manners,
And be more modefter in thy tearmes,
For my unfeined griefe is not to be ruled by thy flattering
And diffembling talke, thou fayeft I am changed,
So I am indeed, and fo muft thou be and that quickly,
Or elfe I muft caufe thee to be chaunged.

Jockey.

Gogs wounds how like you this?
Sownds, tis not fo fweet as muficke.

Tom.

I truft we have not offended your Grace no way.

                           Henry

Henry 5.

Ah *Tom*, your former life grieves me,
And makes me to abandon and abolifh your company for ever,
And therefore not upon pain of death to approch my prefence
By ten miles fpace, then if I heare well of you,
It may bee I will doe fomewhat for you,
Otherwife looke for no more favour at my hands,
Then at any other mans : and therefore be gone,
We have other matters to talke on.   [*Exeunt Knights.*
Now my good Lord Archbifhop of *Canterbury*,
What fay you to our embaffage into *France* ?

Archbifhop.

Your right to the French crowne of *France*,
Came by your great grandmother *Izabel*,
Wife to king *Edward* the third,
And fifter to *Charles* the French King:
Now if the French King deny it, as likely he will,
Then muft you take your fword in hand,
And conquer the right.
Let the ufurped Frenchman know,
Although your predeceffors have let it paffe, you will not :
For your Countreymen are willing with purfe and men,
To ayde you.
Then my good Lord, as it hath been alwayes knowne,
That *Scotland* hath been in league with *France*,
By a fort of penfions which yearly come from thence,
I thinke it therefore beft to conquere *Scotland*,
And then I thinke that you may go more eafily into *France* :
And this is all that I can fay, my good Lord.

Henry 5.

I thanke you, my good L. Archbifhop of *Canterbury*.
What fay you, my good Lord of *Oxford ?*

Oxford.

And pleafe your Majeftie,
I agree to my Lord Archbyfhop, faving in this,
He that will *Scotland* winne, muft firft with *France* beginne :
According to the old faying.
Therefore my good Lord, I thinke it beft firft to invade *France*,
For in conquering *Scotland*, you conquer but one.
And conquere *France*, and conquere both.

Exeter

Enter Lord of Exceter.

Exeter.

And pleefe your Majefty.

Henry 5.

Now truft me my Lord,
He was the laft man that we talked of,
I am glad that he is come to refolve us of our anfwere,
Commit him to our prefence.

Enter Duke of Yorke.

Yorke.

God fave the life of my foveraigne Lord the King.

Henry 5.

Now my good Lord the duke of *Yorke*,
What newes from our brother the French king ?

Yorke.

And pleafe your Majeftie,
I delivered him my embaffage,
Whereof I tooke fome deliberation,
But for the anfwere he hath fent
My Lord Embaffador of *Burges*, the Duke of *Burgony*,
Monfieur le Cole, with two hundred and fiftie horfemen,
To bring the embaffage.

Henry 5.

Commit my Lord Archbyfhop of *Burges* unto our prefence.

Enter Archbyfhop of Burges.

Henry 5.

Now my Lord Archbyfhop of *Burges*,
We doe learne by our Lord Embaffador,
That you haye our meffage to doo
From our brother the French king :
Here my good Lord, according to our accuftomed order,
We give you free libertie and licenfe to fpeake,
With good audience.

Archbyfhop.

God fave the mighty king of *England*,
My Lord and Mafter, the moft Chriftian King,
Charles the feventh, the great and mighty king of *France*,
As a moft noble and Chriftian king,

5   Not

Not minding to fhed innocent bloud, is rather content
To yeeld fomewhat to your unreafonable demaunds,
That if fifty thoufand crownes a yeare with his daughter
The fayde Lady *Katheren*, in marriage,
And fome crownes which he may well fpare,
Not hurting of his kingdome,
He is content to yeeld fo far to your unreafonable defire.

Henry 5.

Why then belike your Lord and Mafter,
Thinkes to puffe me up with fifty thoufand crowns a yere:
No, tell thy Lord and Mafter,
That all the crownes in *France* fhall not ferve me,
Except the crowne and kingdome it felfe:
And perchance hereafter I will have his daughter.

Archbyfhop.

And it pleafe your Majefty,
My Lord Prince *Dolphin* greetes you well,
With this prefent.

[*He delivereth a Tunne of Tennis balles.*
Henry 5.

What a guilded tunne?
I pray you my Lord of *Yorke*, looke what is in it.

Yorke.

And it pleafe your Grace,
Here is a Carpet, and a Tunne of Tennis balles.

Henry 5.

A tunne of tennis balles?
I pray you good my Lord Archbifhop,
What might the meaning thereof be?

Archbyfhop.

And it pleafe you my Lord,
A meffenger you know ought to keepe clofe his meffage,
And fpecially an embaffador.

Henry 5.

But I know that you may declare your meffage
To a king, the law of armes allowes no leffe.

Archbyfhop.

My Lord, hearing of your wildneffe before your
Fathers death, fent you this my good Lord,

Meaning

Meaning that you are more fitter for a Tennis Court
Then a field, and more fitter for a Carpet then the Campe.

Henry 5.

My L. Prince *Dolphin* is very pleasant with me:
But tell him, that in steed of balles of leather,
We will tosse him balles of brasse and yron,
Yea, such balles, as never were tost in *France*,
The proudest Tennis Court shall rue it,
I, and thou Prince of *Burges* shall rue it.
Therefore get thee hence, and tell him thy massage quickly
Least I be there before thee: Away priest, be gone.

Archbyshop.

I beseech your Grace, to deliver mee your safe
Conduct under your broad seale Emanuel.   ×

Henry 5.

Priest of *Burges*, know,
That the hand and seale of a King, and his word is all one,
And in stead of my hand and seale,
I will bring him my hand and sword.
And tell thy Lord and Master, that I *Harry* of *England* said it.
And I *Harry* of *England*, will performe it.
My Lord of *Yorke*, deliver him our safe conduct,
Under our broad seale Emanuel.   ×

[Exeunt Archbishop and the Duke of Yorke.

Now my Lords, to Armes, to Armes,
For I vow by heaven and earth, that the proudest
French man in all *France* shall rue the time that ever
These tennis balles were sent into *England.*
My Lord, I wil that there be provided a great navy of ships
With all speed, at *South-Hampton.*
For there I meane to ship my men,
For I would be there before him, if it were possible,
Therefore come; but stay,
I had almost forgot the chiefest thing of all, with chasing
With this French embassadour.
Call in my Lord Chiefe Justice of *England.*

Enter Lord Chiefe Justice of England.

Exeter.

Here is the King, my Lord.

Justice.

Juftice.

God preferve your Majefty.

Henry 5.

Why how now my Lord, what is the matter?

Juftice.

I would it were unknowne to your Majefty.

Henry 5.

Why what ayle you?

Juftice.

Your Majefty knoweth my griefe well.

Henry 5.

Oh my Lord, you remember you fent me to the Fleet, did you not.

Juftice.

I truft your Grace hath forgotten that.

Henry 5.

I truly my Lord, and for revengement,
I have chofen you to be my Protector over my realme,
Untill it fhall pleafe God to give me fpeedy returne
Out of *France*.

Juftice.

And if it pleafe your Majefty, I am farre unworthy
Of fo high a dignity.

Henry 5.

Tut my Lord, you are not unworthy,
Becaufe I thinke you worthy:
For you that would not fpare me,
I thinke will not fpare another.
It muft needs be fo, and therefore come,
Let us be gone, and get our men in a readineffe.   [*Exeunt.*

Enter a Captaine, John Cobler *and his Wife.*

Captaine.

Come, come, there is no remedy,
Thou muft needs ferve the King.

John.

Good mafter Captaine let me goe,
I am not able to go fo farre.

Wife.

I pray you good mafter Captaine,
P e good to my hufband.

Captaine.

Captaine.

Why I am fure he is not too good to ferve the King:

John.

Alaffe no : but a great deale too bad,
Therefore I pray you let me go.

Captaine.

No, no, thou fhalt go.

John.

Oh fir, I have a great many fhooes at home for to cobble.

Wife.

I pray you let him goe home againe.

Captaine.

Tufh I care not, thou fhalt goe.

Wife.

Oh wife, and you had been a loving wife to mee,
This had not been, for I have fayd many times,
That I would goe away, and now I muft goe
Againft my will.   [*Hee weepeth.*

Enters Dericke.

Dericke.

How now ho, *Bafillus manus*, for an old codpeece,
Mafter Captaine fhall we away :
Sowndes how now *John*, what a crying,
What make you and my dame there?
I marvell whofe head you will throw the ftooles at,
Now we are gone.

Wife.

Ile tell you, come ye cloghead,
What doe you with my potlid? heare you,
Will you have it rapt about your pate?
                        [*She beateth him with her potlid.*

Dericke.

Oh good dame.   [*Here he fhakes her.*
And I had my dagger here, I would worie you all to peeces
That I would.

Wife.

Would you fo, Ile trie that.   [*She beateth him.*

Dericke.

Mafter Captaine will yee fuffer her?
Goe too dame, I will goe backe as farre as I can,

Z.   But

But and you come againe,
Ile clap the Law on your backe thats flat :
Ile tell you Mafter Captaine what you fhall doe;
Preffe her for a fouldier, I warrant you,
She wil doe as much good as her hufband and I too.

Enters the Theefe.

Sownes, who comes yonder ?

Captaine.

How now good fellow, doeft thou want a Mafter ?

Theefe.

I truly fir.

Captaine.

Hold thee then, I preffe thee for a fouldier,
To ferve the King in *France.*

Dericke.

How now Gads, what doeft, knoweft, thinkeft?

Theefe.

I, I knew thee long agoe.

Dericke.

Heare you maifter Captaine ?

Captaine.

What fayft thou ?

Dericke.

I pray you let me goe home againe.

Captaine.

Why what woldft thou doe at home ?

Dericke.

Marry I have brought two fhirts with me,
And I would carry one of them home againe,
For I am fure heele fteale it from me,
He is fuch a filching fellow.

Captaine.

I warrant thee hee will not fteale it from thee,
Come lets away. .

Dericke.

Come maifter Captaine lets away,
Come follow me.

John.

Come Wife, lets part lovingly.

Wife.

Wife.

Farewell good hufband.

Dericke.

Fye what a kiffing and crying is here?
Sownes, do ye thinke he will never come againe?
Why *John* come away, doeſt thinke that we are ſo baſe
Minded to die among Frenchmen?
Sownes, we know not whether they will lay
Us in their Church or no: Come, M. Captaine, lets away.

Captaine.

I cannot ſtay no longer, therefore come away.

[*Exeunt omnes.*

Enter the King, Prince Dolphin, *and Lord High Conſtable of*
France.

King.

Now my Lord High Conſtable,
What ſay you to our Embaſſage into *England?*

Conſtable.

And it pleafe your Majeſtie, I can ſay nothing,
Untill my Lords Embaſſadors be come home,
But yet me thinkes your grace hath done well,
To get your men in ſo good a readineſſe,
For feare of the worſt.

King.

I my Lord we have ſome in a readineſſe,
But if the King of *England* make againſt us,
We muſt have thrice ſo many moe.

Dolphin.

Tut my Lord, although the King of *England* be
Young and wilde headed, yet never thinke hee will be ſo
Unwife to make battell againſt the mightie King of
France.

King.

Oh my ſonne, although the King of *England* be
Young and wilde headed, yet never thinke but he is rulde
By his wife Councellors.

Enter Archbyſhop of Burges.

Archbyſhop.

God fave the life of my ſoveraigne lord the King.

Z 2

King.

King.

Now my good Lord Archbifhop of *Burges,*
What newes from our brother the Englifh King ?
Archbyfhop.

And pleafe your Majeftie,
He is fo far from your expectation,
That nothing will ferve him but the Crowne
And Kingdome it felfe ; befides, he bad me hafte quickly,
Leaft hee be there before mee, and fo farre as I heare
He hath kept promife: for they fay he is already landed
At *Kidcocks* in *Normandie,* upon the River of *Sene,*
And layd his fiege to the Garrifon Towne of *Harflew.*

King.

You have made great hafte in the meane time,
Have you not ?

Dolphin.

I pray you my Lord, how did the King of
England take my prefents ?

Archbyfhop.

Truely my Lord, in very ill part,
For thefe your balles of leather,
He will toffe you balles of braffe and yron.
Truft me my Lord, I was verie affraide of him,
Hee is fuch a hautie and high minded Prince,
He is as fierce as a Lyon.

Conftable.

Tufh, we will make him as tame as a lambe,
I warrant you.

Enters a Meffenger.

Meffenger.

God fave the mightie King of *France.*

King.

Now Meffenger, what newes ?

Meffenger.

And it pleafe your Majeftie
I come from your poore diftreffed Towne of *Harflew,*
Which is fo befet on every fide,
If your Majeftie doe not fend prefent ayde,
The Towne will be yeelded to the *Englifh King.*

King.

King.

Come my Lords, come, ſhall we ſtand ſtill
Till our Countrey be ſpoyled under our noſes ?
My Lords, let the *Normans, Brabants, Pickardies,*
And *Danes,* be ſent for with all ſpeede :
And you my Lord High Conſtable, I make Generall
Over all my whole Armie.
Monſieur le Colle, Maiſter of the Boas,
Signior Devcns, and the reſt, at your appointment.

Dolphin.

I truſt your Majeſtie will beſtow,
Some part of the battell on mee,
I hope not to preſent any otherwiſe then well.

King.

I tell thee my ſonne,
Although I ſhould get the victory, and thou loſe thy life,
I ſhould thinke my ſelfe quite conquered,
And the *Engliſhmen* to have the victorie.

Dolphin.

Why my Lord and Father,
I would have the pettie King of *England* to know,
That I dare encounter him in any ground of the world.

King.

I know well my ſonne,
But at this time I will have it thus :
Therefore come away.   [*Exeunt omnes.*

Enters Henry *the fifth, with his Lordes.*

Henry 5.

Come my Lords of *England,*
No doubt this good lucke of winning this Towne
Is a ſigne of an honourable victorie to come.
But good my Lord, go and ſpeak to the Captaines
With all ſpeed, to number the hoaſt of the French men.
And by that meanes we may the better know
How to appoint the battell.

Yorke.

And it pleaſe your Majeſty,
There are many of your men ſicke and diſeaſed,
And many of them die for want of victuals.

Z 3   *Henry*

Henry 5.
And why did you not tell me of it before?
If we cannot have it for money,
We will have it by dint of fword.
The law of armes allow no leffe.

Oxford.
I befeech yur grace, to grant me a boone.

Henry 5.
What is that my good Lord?

Oxford.
That your grace would give me the Evantgard in the battell,

Henry 5.
Truft me my Lord cf *Oxford* I cannot:
For I have already given it to my unckle the Duke of *Yorke*,
Yet I thanke you for your good will.   [*A Trumpet founds,*
How now, what is that?

Yorke.
I thinke it be fome Herald of armes.

Enters a Herald.

Herald.
King of *England*, my Lord High Conftable,
And others of the Noble men of *France*,
Sends me to defie thee, as open enemy to God,
Our Countrey, and us, and hereupon,
They prefently bid thee battell.

Henry 5.
Herald, tell them, that I defie them,
As open enemies to God, my Countrey, and me,
And as wrongful ufurpers of my right:
And whereas thou fayeft they prefently bid me battell,
Tell them that I thinke they know how to pleafe me:
But I pray thee what place hath my Lord Prince *Dolphin*
Here in battell.

Herald.
And it pleafe your Grace,
My Lord and King his father
Will not let him come into the field.

Henry 5.
Why then he doth me great injury,
I thought that he and I fhuld have plaid at tennis together,
                                    Therefore

Therefore I have brought tennis balles for him,
But other manner of ones then he sent me.
And Herald, tell my Lord Prince *Dolphin*,
That I have inured my hands with other kind of weapons
Then tennis balles, ere this time a day,
And that he shall finde it, ere it be long,
And so adue my friend :
And tell my Lord that I am ready when he will.   [*Exit Herald.*
Come my Lords, I care not and I go to our Captaines,
And ile fee the number of the French army my felfe.
Strike up the drumme.   [*Exeunt omnes.*

Enter French Souldiers.

1 *Souldier.*

Come away Jacke Drummer, come away all,
And me will tell you, what me will doo,
Me will tro one chance on the dice,
Who shall have the king of *England* and his Lords.

2 *Souldier.*

Come away Jacke Drummer,
And tro your chance, and lay downe your Drumme.

Enter Drummer.

Drummer.

Oh the brave apparrell that the English mans
Hay broth over, I will tell you what
Me ha done, me ha provided a hundreth trunkes,
And all to put the fine parel of the English mans in.

1 *Souldier.*

What doe you meane by trunkea ?

2 *Souldier.*

A sheft man, a hundred shefts.

1 *Shouldier.*

Awee, awee, awee, Me will tell you what,
Me ha put five shildren out of my house,
And all too little to put the fine apparrell of the
English mans in.

Drummer.

Oh the brave the brave apparrell that wee shall have anon,
but come, and you shall fee what me will tro at the Kings
Drummer and Fife.

Z 4   Ha,

Ha, me ha no good lucke, tro you.

3 Souldier.

Faith me will tro at the Earle of *Northumberland*
And my Lord a *Willowbie*, with his great horfe,
Snorting, farting, oh brave horfe.

1 Souldier.

Ha, bur Lady you ha reafonable good lucke,
Now I will tro at the King himfelfe,
Ha, me have no good lucke.

Enters a Captaine.

Captaine.

How now what make you here,
So farre from the campe?

2 Souldier.

Shal me tell our captain, what we have done here.

Drummer.

Awee, awee.   [*Exeunt Drum and one Souldier.*

2 Souldier.

I will tell you what we have done,
We have been troing on fhance on the dice,
But none can win the King.

Captaine.

I thinke fo, why he is left behind for mee
And I have fet three or foure chaire makers a worke,
To make a new difguifed chaire to fet that womanly King of
England in, that all the people may laugh and fcoffe at him.

2 Souldier.

O brave Captaine.

Captaine.

I am glad and yet with a kind of pitty,
To fee the poore King.
Who ever faw a more flourifhing armie in *France* in one
day then here is. Are not here all the Peeres of *France*:
Are not here the Normans with their fieric hand Gunnes,
and flaunching Curtleaxes.
Are not here the Barbarians with their bard horfes, and lanch-
ing fpeares?
Are not here Pickardes with their Crofbows and piercing Darts?
The Henves with their cutting Glaves, and fharpe Carbuckles?
Are not here the Lance Knights of Burgundie?

And

And on the other fide, a fite of poore Englifh fcabs ?
Why take an Englifh man out of his warme bed,
And his ftale drinke but one moneth,
And alaffe, what will become of him ?
But give the Frenchman a Reddifh root,
And he will live with it all the days of his life.   [*Exit.*

2 *Souldier.*

Oh the brave apparrell that we fhall have of the Englifh mans.
[*Exit.*

Enters the King of England, *and his Lords.*

Henry 5.

Come my Lords and fellowes of Armes,
What company is there of the French men ?

Oxford.

And it pleafe your Majefty,
Our Captaines have numbred them,
And fo neare as they can judge,
They are about threefcore thoufand horfemen,
And forty thoufand footmen.

Henry 5.

They threefcore thoufand,
And we but two thoufand.
They threefcore thoufand footmen,
And we twelve thoufand.
They are a hundred thoufand,
And we forty thoufand, ten to one.
My Lords and loving Countrey men,
Though we be few, and they many,
Feare not, your quarrell is good, and God will defend you :
Plucke up your hearts, for this day we fhall eyther have
A valiant victory, or an honourable death.
Now my Lords, I will that my uncle the Duke of *Yorke,*
Have the avantgard in the hartell.
The Earle of *Darby,* the Earle of *Oxford,*
The Earle of *Kent,* the Earle of *Nottingham,*
The Earle of *Huntington,* I will have befide the army,
That they may come frefh upon them.
And I my felfe with the Duke of *Bedford,*
The Duke of *Clarence,* and the Duke of *Glofter,*
Will be in the midft of the battell.

Furthermore,

Furthermore, I will that my Lord of *Willowbie*,
And the Earl of *Northumberland*,
With their troupes of horfemen, be continually running like
wings on both fides of the army:
My Lord of *Northumberland*, on the left wing.
Then I will that every archer provide him a ftake of a tree, and
ſharpe it at both ends.
And at the firft encounter of the horfemen,
To pitch their ftakes downe into the ground before them,
That they may gore themfelves upon them,
And then to recoyle backe, and ſhoot wholly altogether.
And fo difcomfite them.

Oxford.

And it pleafe your Majefty,
I will take that in charge, if your Grace be therwith content.

Henry 5.

With all my heart, my good Lord of *Oxford*.
And go and provide quickly.

Oxford.

I thanke your Highneffe.   [*Exit.*

Henry 5.

Well my Lords, our battels are ordayned,
And the French making bonfires, and at their banquets,
But let them looke, for I meane to fet upon them.

[*The Trumpet founds.*

Soft, here comes fome other French meffage.

Enters Herauld.

Herald.

King of *England*, my Lord High Conftable,
And other of my Lords, confidering the poor eftate of thee
And thy poore Countrey men,
Sends me to know what thou wilt give for thy ranfome?
Perhaps thou mayeft agree better cheape now,
Then when thou art conquered.

Henry 5.

Why then belike your High Conftable,
Sends to know what I will give for my Ranfome?
Now truft me Herald, not fo much as a tun of Tenis-balls,
No not fo much as one poore Tennis-ball:
Rather ſhall my body lie dead in the Field to feed crowes,

Then

Then ever *England* fhall pay one penny ranfome
For my bodie.
                                    Herald.
  A Kingly refolution.
                                    Henry 5.
  No Herald, tis a Kingly refolution,
And the refolution of a King :
Here take this for thy paines.   [*Exit Herald.*
But ftay my Lords, what time is it ?
                                    All.
  Prime my Lord.
                                    Henry 5.
  Then it is good time no doubt,
For all *England* prayeth for us :
What my Lords, me thinks you looke cheerfully upon me ?
Why then with one voyce, and like true Englifh hearts,
With me throw up your caps. and for *England.*
Crie S. *George*, and God and S. *George belpe us.*
                       [*Strike Drummes.   Exeunt omnes.*

¶ *The French-men cry within, S. Dennis, S. Dennis, Mount,*
    Joy, Saint Dennis.

                    The Battell.

    Enters King of England, and his Lords.

                                    Henry 5.
  Come my Lords, come, by this time our
Swords are almoft drunke with French bloud,
But my Lordes, which of you can tell me how many of our
Armie be flaine in the Battell ?
                                    Oxford.
  And it pleafe your Majeftie,
There are of the French Armie flaine,
Above ten thoufand, twentie fixe hundred
Whereof are Princes and Nobles bearing Banners :
Befides, all the Nobilitie of *France* are taken prifoners.
Of your Majeftie Armie, are flaine none but the good
Duke of *Yorke*, and not above five or fixe and twentie
Common fouldiours.
                                    Henry 5.
  For the good Duke of *Yorke* my Unckle,
I am heartily forrie, and greatly lament his misfortune,
                                                    Yet

Yet the honourable victorie which the Lord hath given us,
Doth make me much rejoyce.   But ftay,
Here comes another French meffage.   [*Sound Trumpet.*

Enters a Herauld, and kneeleth.

Herald.

God fave the life of the moft mightie Conqueror,
The honourable King of *England?*

Henry 5.

Now Herald, me thinks the world is changed
With you now : what? I am fure it is a great difgrace for a
Herald to kneele to the King of *England.*
What is thy meffage?

Herald.

My Lord and Maifter, the conquered King of *France*
Sends thee long health, with heartie greeting.

Henry 5.

Herald his greetings are welcome,
But I thanke God for my health :
Well Herald, fay on.

Herald.

He hath fent me to defire your Majeftie,
To give him leave to goe into the field to view his poore
Countrey-men, that they may all be honourably buried.

Henry 5.

Why Herald, doth thy Lord and Mafter
Send to me to bury the dead,
Let him bury them a Gods name.
But I pray thee Herald, where is my Lord High Conftable,
And thofe that would have had my ranfome?

Herald.

And it pleafe your Majeftie,
He was flaine in the battell.

Henry 5.

Why you may fee, you will make your felves
Sure before the victory be wonne : but Herald,
What Caftle is this, fo neere adjoyning to our Campe?

Herald.

And it pleafe your Majeftie,
Tis calde the Caftle of *Agincourt.*

Henry

Henry 5.

Well then my Lords of *England*,
For the more honour of our Englifhmen,
I will that this be for ever calde the battell of *Agincourt.*

Herald.

And it pleafe your Majefty,
I have a further meffage to deliver to your Majefty.

Henry 5.

What is that, Herald? fay on.

Herald.

And it pleafe your Majefty, my Lord and Mafter,
Craves to parley with your Majefty.

Henry 5.

With a good will, fo fome of my Nobles
View the place for feare of trechery and treafon.

Herald.

Your Grace needs not to doubt that.   [*Exit Herald*

Henry 5.

Well, tell him then I will come.
Now my Lords, I will goe into the field my felfe,
To view my Countrey men, and to have them honourably
buried, for the French King fhall never furpaffe me in curtefie,
whiles I am *Harry* King of England.
Come on my Lords.   [*Exeunt omnes.*

Enter John Cobler, *and* Robin Pewterer.

Robin.

Now, *John Cobler,*
Didft thou fee how the King did behave himfelfe?

John.

But *Robin*, didft thou fee what a policy
The King had, to fee how the French men were kilde
With the ftakes of the trees.

Robin.

I *John*, there was a brave policie.

Enters an Englifh *Souldier roming.*

Souldier.

What are you my mafters?

Both.

Why we be Englifhmen.

3   *Souldier.*

Souldier.

Are you Englifh men, then change your language,
For all the Kings tents are fet a fire,
And all they that fpeake Englifh will be kilde.

John.

What fhall we do *Robin*, faith ile fhift,
For I can fpeake broken French.

Robin.

Faith fo can I, lets heare how thou canft fpeake?

John.

Commodcvales Monfieur.

Robin.

Thats well, come lets be gone.   [*Drum and Trumpets found.*]

Enter Dericke *roming.   After him a* Frenchman, *and takes him
prifoner.*

Dericke.

O good *Mounfer.*

French-man.

Come, come, you *villcaco.*

Dericke.

O I will fir, I will.

Frenchman.

Come quickly you pefant.

Dericke.

I will fir, what fhall I give you?

Frenchman.

Marry thou fhalt give me,
One, to, tre, foure hundred Crownes.

Dericke.

Nay fir, I will give you more,
I will give you as many crownes as will lye on your fword.

Frenchman.

Wilt thou give me as many crownes
As will lye on my fword?

Dericke.

I marrie will I, I but you muft lay downe your
Sword, or elfe they will not lye on your fword.
[*Here the Frenchman layes downe his Sword, and the Clowne takes
it up, and hurles him downe.*

Dericke.

Dericke.

Thou villaine, dareſt thou looke up?

Frenchman.

O good *Monſieur comparteve.*
Monſieur, pardon me.

Dericke.

O you villaine, now you lye at my mercy,
Doeſt thou remember ſince thou lambſt me in thy ſhort el?
O villaine, now I will ſtrike off thy head.

[*Here while he turnes his backe, the Frenchman runnes his wayes.*

Dericke.

What is he gone, maſſe I am glad of it,
For if he had ſtaid, I was afraid he would have ſturd againe
And then I ſhould have beene ſpilt,
But I will away, to kill more Frenchmen.

Enters King of France, *King of* England, *and attendants.*

Henry 5.

Now my good brother of *France,*
My coming into this land was not to ſhed bloud,
But for the right of my Countrey, which if you can deny,
I am content peaceably to leave my ſiege,
And to depart out of your land.

Charles.

What is your demaund,
My loving brother of *England?*

Henry 5.

My Secretary hath it written, read it.

Secretary.

Item, that immediately *Henry* of *England*
Be crowned King of *France.*

Charles.

A very hard ſentence,
My good brother of *England.*

Henry 5.

No more but right, my good brother of *France.*

French King.

Well, read on.

Secretary.

Item, that after the death of the ſaid *Henry,*
The Crowne remaine to him and his heyres for ever.

7   *French*

French King.

Why then you doe not onely meane to difpoffeffe me, but
alfo my fonne.

Henry 5.

Why my good brother of *France*,
You have had it long inough :
And as for Prince *Dolphin*,
It fkils not though he fit befide the faddle :
Thus I have fet it downe, and thus it fhall be.

French King.

You are very peremptory,
My good brother of *England*.

Henry 5.

And you as perverfe, my good brother of *France*.

Charles.

Why then belike all that I have here is yours.

Henry 5.

I even as farre as the kingdom of *France* reaches.

Charles.

I for by this hote beginning,
We fhall fcarce bring it to a calme ending.

Henry 5.

It is as you pleafe, here is my refolution.

Charles.

Well my brother of *England*,
If you will give me a coppy,
We will meet you againe to morrow.

[*Exit King of* France, *and all their attendants.*

Henry 5.

With a good will my good brother of *France*,
Secretary deliver him a Copie,
My Lords of *England* goe before,
And I will follow you.   [*Exeunt Lords.*

Henry 5.   [*Speakes to himfelfe.*

Ah *Harry*, thrice unhappy *Harry*,
Haft thou now conquerd the French King,
And begins a frefh fupply with his daughter,
But with what face canft thou feeke to gaine her love,
Which haft fought to win her fathers Crowne ?

Her

Her fathers Crowne faid I, no it is mine owne:
I but I love her, and muft crave her,
Nay I love her, and will have her.

Enters Lady Katheren *and her Ladies.*

But here fhee comes:
How now fayre Lady *Katheren* of *France*,
What newes?

Katheren.

And it pleafe your Majefty,
My father fent me to know if you will debate any of thefe
Unreafonable demands, which you require.

Henry 5.

Now truft me *Kate*,
I commend thy fathers wit greatly in this,
For none in the world could fooner have made me debate it,
If it were poffible:
But tell me fweet *Kate*, canft thou tell how to love.

Kate.

I cannot hate my good Lord,
Therefore farre unfit were it for me to love.

Henry 5.

Tufh *Kate*, but tell me in plaine termes,
Canft thou love the King of *England?*
I cannot doe as thefe Countries doe,
That fpend halfe their time in wooing:
Tufh wench, I am none fuch.
But wilt thou go over to *England?*

Kate.

I would to God, that I had your Majefty,
As faft in love, as you have my father in warres,
I would not vouchfafe fo much as one looke,
Untill you had related all thefe unreafonable demaunds.

Henry 5.

Tufh *Kate*, I know thou wouldft not ufe mee fo hardly:
but tell me, canft thou love the King of *England?*

Kate.

How fhould I love him, that hath dealt fo hardly with my
father?

Henry

Henry 5.

But ile deale as eafily with thee,
As thy heart can imagine, or tongue require,
How fayft thou, what will it be?

Kate.

If I were of my owne direction,
I could give you anfwere:
But feeing I ftand at my fathers direction,
I muft firft know his will.

Henry 5.

But fhall I have thy good will in the mean feafon?

Kate.

Whereas I can put your Grace in no affurance,
I would be loath to put your Grace in any defpayre.

Henry 5.

Now before God, it is a fweet wench.

[She goes afide, and fpeakes as followeth.

Kate.

I may thinke my felfe the happieft in the world,
That is beloved of the mightie king of *England.*

Henry 5.

Well *Kate*, are you at hoaft with me?
Sweete *Kate*, tell thy father from me,
That none in the world could fooner have perfwaded mee to
it.then thou, and fo tell thy father from me.

Kate.

God keepe your Majefty in good health.   [*Exit Kate.*

Henry 5.

Farewell fweet *Kate*, in faith it is a fweet wench,
But if I knew I could not have her fathers good will,
I would fo rowfe the Towers over his eares,
That I would make him be glad to bring her me,
Upon his hands and knees.   [*Exit King.*

Enters Dericke *with his girdle full of fhooes.*

Dericke.

How now? Sownes it did me good to fee how I did triumph
over the French men.

Enters

Enters John Cobler *roving, with a packe full of apparrell.*

John.

Whoope *Dericke*, how doeſt thou ?

Dericke.

What *John Comedevales*, alive yet ?

John.

I promiſe thee *Dericke*, I ſcapt hardly,
For I was within halfe a mile when one was kilde.

Dericke.

Were you ſo ?

John.

I truſt me, I had like beene ſlaine.

Dericke.

But once kilde, why it tis nothing,
I was foure or five times ſlaine.

John.

Foure or five times ſlaine.
Why how couldſt thou have beene alive now ?

Dericke.

O *John*, never ſay ſo,
For I was calde the bloudy ſouldier amongſt them all.

John.

Why what didſt thou ?

Dericke.

Why, I will tell thee *John*,
Every day when I went into the field,
I would take a ſtraw, and thruſt it into my noſe,
And make my noſe bleed, and then I would go into the field
And when the Captaine ſaw me, he would ſay,
Peace a bloudy ſouldier, and bid me ſtand aſide,
Whereof I was glad :
But marke the chance *John*.
I went and ſtood behind a tree, but marke then *John*,
I thought I had beene ſafe, but on a ſodaine,
There ſteps to me a luſty tall French-man,
Now he drew, and I drew,
Now I lay here, and he lay there.
Now I ſet this leg before, and turned this backeward,
And ſkipped quite over a hedge,
And he ſaw me no more there that day.
And was not this well done *John?*

A a 2

John.

John.

Maſſe *Dericke,* thou haſt a witty head.

Dericke.

I *John,* thou maiſt ſee, it thou hadſt taken my counſel.
But what haſt thou there?
I thinke thou haſt bene robbing the French-men.

John.

I faith *Dericke,* I have gotten ſome reparrell,
To carry home to my Wife.

Dericke.

And I have got ſome ſhooes,
For I'e tell thee what I did, when they were dead,
I would go take off all theyr ſhooes.

John.

I, but *Dericke,* how ſhall wee get home?

Dericke.

Nay, ſownds and they take thee,
They will hang thee,
O *John,* never doe ſo, if it be thy Fortune to be hangd,
Be hangd in thy cwne language whatſoever thou doeſt.

John.

Why *Dericke* the warres is done,
We may gee home now.

Dericke.

I, but you may not go before you aſke the king leave;
But I know a way to go home, and aſke the king no leave.

John.

How is that *Dericke?*

Dericke.

Why *John,* thou knoweſt the Duke of *Yorkes*
Funerall muſt be carryed into *England,* doeſt thou not?

John.

I, that I doe.

Dericke.

Why then thou knoweſt weele go with it.

John.

I but *Dericke,* how ſhall wee doe for to meet them?

Dericke.

Sownes if I make not ſhift to meet them, hang me.
Syria, thou knoweſt that in every Towne there will

Be ringing, and there will be cakes and drinke:
Now I will goe to the Clarke and Sexton,
And keepe a talking, and fay, O this fellow rings well:
And thou fhalt goe and take a piece of cake, then ile ring,
And thou fhalt fay, Oh this fellow keepes a good ftint,
And then I wil goe drinke to thee all the way:
But I marvell what my dame wil fay when we come home,
Becaufe we have not a French word to caft at a Dog
By the way?

John.
Why what fhall we doe, *Dericke?*
Dericke.
Why *John*, ile goe before, and call my dame whore,
And thou fhalt come after, and fet fire on the houfe.
We may doe it *John*, for ile prove it,
Becaufe we be fouldiers.   [*The Trumpets found.*
John.
Dericke helpe me to carry my fhooes and bootes.

Enters King of England, *L rd of* Oxford, *and* Exceter, *then the*
King of France, *Prince* Dolphin, *and the Duke of* Burgondy,
and attendants.

Henry 5.
Now my good brother of *France*,
I hope by this time you have deliberated of your anfwere.
French King.
I my wel beloved brother of *England*,
We have viewed it over with our learned Councell,
But cannot finde that you fhould be crowned
King of *France.*
Henry 5.
What not King of *France*, then nothing,
I muft be king: but my loving brother of *France*,
I can hardly forget the late injuries offered me,
When I came laft to parley,
The French men had better a raked
The bowels out of their fathers carkaffes,
Then to have fiered my Tentes.
· And if I knew thy fonne Prince *Dolphin* for one,
I would fo rowfe him, as he was never fo rowfed.

French

French King.

I dare fweare for my fonnes Innocency in this matter,
But if this pleafe you, that immediately you be
Proclaimed and crowned Heyre and Regent of *France*,
Not king, becaufe I my felfe was once crowned king,

Henry 5.

Heyre and Regent of *France*, that is well,
But that is not all that I muft have.

French King.

The reft my Secretary hath in writing.

Secretary.

Item, that *Henry* king of *England*,
Be·crowned Heyre and Regent of *France*,
During the life of king *Charles*, and after his death,
The Crowne with all rights, to remaine to King *Henry*
Of *England*, and to his heyres for ever.

Henry 5.

Well, my good brother of *France*,
There is one thing I muft needs defire.

French King.

What is that, my good brother of *England?*

Henry 5.

That all your Nobles muft be fworne to be true to me.

French King.

Whereas they have not ftucke with greater matters, I know
they will not fticke with fuch a trifle,
Beginne you my Lord Duke of *Burgondie*.

Henry 5.

Come, my Lord of *Burgondie*,
Take your oath upon my fword.

Burgondie.

I *Philip* Duke of *Burgondie*,
Sweare to *Henry* King of *England*,
To be true to him, and to become his league-man,
And that if I *Philip* heare of any forraigne power,
Comming to invade the fayde *Henry*, or his heyres,
Then I the fayde *Philip* to fend him word,
And ayde him with all the power I can make,
And thereunto I take my oath.   [*He kiffeth the fword.*

3   *Henry*

Henry 5.

Come, Prince *Dolphin*, you muſt ſweare too.

[*He kiſſeth the ſword.*

Henry 5.

Well, my brother of *France*,

There is one thing more I muſt needs require of you.

French King.

Wherein is it that we may ſatisfie your Majeſtie?

Henry 5.

A trifle my good brother of *France.*

I meane to make your daughter Queene of *England*,

If ſhe be willing, and you therewith content:

How ſayſt thou *Kate*, canſt thou love the King of *England*?

Kate.

How ſhould I love thee, which is my fathers enemie?

Henry 5.

Tut ſtand not upon theſe points,

Tis you muſt make us friends:

I know *Kate*, thou art not a little proud, that I love thee,

What wench, the king of *England*.

French King.

Daughter let nothing ſtand betwixt the king of *England*

and thee, agree to it.

Kate.

I had beſt whilſt he is willing,

Leſt when I would, he will not,

I reſt at your Majeſties commaund.

Henry 5.

Welcome ſweet *Kate*, but my brother of *France*

What ſay you to it?

French King.

With all my heart I like it,

But when ſhall be your wedding day?

Henry 5.

The firſt Sunday of the next moneth,

God willing.   [*Sound Trumpets.*

[*Exeunt omnes.*

F I N I S.

THE TRUE

CHRONICLE HISTORY

OF

KING LEIR,

AND

HIS THREE DAUGHTERS,

GONORILL, RAGAN, and CORDELLA.

As it hath bene divers and ſundry times lately acted.

London, Printed by SIMON STAFFORD for JOHN WRIGHT, and are to bee ſold at his ſhop at Chriſtes church dore, next *Newgate-market,* 1605.

B b

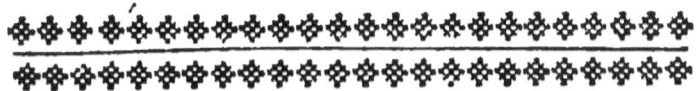

THE TRUE

CHRONICLE HISTORIE

OF

K I N G   L E I R,

AND HIS

THREE DAUGHTERS.

A C T U S   I.

Enter king Leir *and nobles.*

THUS to our griefe the obfequies performd
    Of our (too late) deceaft and deareft queen,
Whofe foule I hope, poffeft of heavenly joyes,
Doth ride in triumph 'mongft the cherubins;
Let us requeft your grave advice, my lords,
For the difpofing of our princely daughters,
For whom our care is fpecially imployd,
As nature bindeth to advance their ftates,
In royal marriage with fome princely mates:
For wanting now their mothers good advice,
Under whofe government they have received
A perfit patterne of a vertuous life:
Left as it were a fhip without a ftcrne,
Or filly fheepe without a paftors care;
Although our felves doe dearely tender them,

Yet

Yet are we ignorant of their affayres :
For fathers beſt do know to governe ſonnes ;
But daughters ſteps the mothers counſel turnes.
A ſonne we want for to ſucceed our crowne,
And courſe of time hath cancelled the date
Of further iſſue from our withered loines :
One foote already hangeth in the grave,
And age hath made deepe furrowes in my face :
The world of me, I of the world am weary,
And I would faine reſigne theſe earthly cares,
And thinke upon the welfare of my ſoule :
Which by no better meanes may be effected,
Then by reſigning up the crowne from me.
In equal dowry to my daughters three.

        Skalliger.
    A worthy care, my liege, which well declares,
The zeale you bare unto our *quondam* queene :
And ſince your grace hath licens'd me to ſpeake,
I cenſure thus ; your majeſty knowing well,
What ſeveral ſuters your princely daughters have,
To make them eche a jointer more or leſſe,
As is their worth, to them that love profeſſe.

        Leir.
    No more, nor leſſe, but even all alike,
My zeale is fixt, all faſhiond in one mould :
Wherefore unpartial ſhall my cenſure be,
Both old and young ſhall have alike for me.

        Nobles.
    My gracious lord, I hartily do wiſh,
That God hath lent you an heire indubitate,
Which might have ſet upon your royal throne,
When fates ſhould looſe the priſon of your life,
By whoſe ſucceſſion all this doubt might ceaſe ;
And as by you, by him we might have peace.
But after-wiſhes ever come too late,
And nothing can revoke the courſe of fate :
Wherefore, my liege, my cenſure deemes it beſt,
To match them with ſome of your neighbour kings,
Bordring within the bounds of *Albion*,

                                By

By whofe united friendſhip, this our ſtate
May be protected 'gainſt all forraine hate.
Leir.
    Herein, my lords, your wiſhes fort with mine,
And mine (I hope) do fort with heavenly powers:
For at this inſtant two neere neighbouring kings,
Of *Cornwall* and of *Cambria*, motion love
To my two daughters, *Gonorill* and *Ragan.*
My youngeſt daughter, faire *Cordella*, vowes
No liking to a monarch, unleſſe love allowes.
She is follicited by divers peeres;
But none of them her partiall fancy heares.
Yet, if my policy may her beguile,
Ile match her to fome king within this ile,
And fo eſtabliſh ſuch a perfit peace,
As fortunes force ſhall ne're prevaile to ceaſe.
Perillus.
    Of us and ours, your gracious care, my lord,
Deferves an everlaſting memory,
To be inrol'd in chronicles of fame,
By never-dying perpetuity:
Yet to become fo provident a prince,
Lofe not the title of a loving father:
Do not force love, where fancy cannot dwell,
Left ſtreames being ſtopt, above the banks do ſwell.
Leir.
    I am refolv'd, and even now my mind
Doth meditate a fudden ſtratagem,
To try which of my daughters loves me beſt:
Which till I know, I cannot be in reſt.
This graunted, when they jointly ſhall contend,
Eche to exceed the other in their love:
Then at the vantage will I take *Cordella*,
Even as ſhe doth proteſt ſhe loves me beſt,
Ile fay, then, daughter, graunt me one requeſt,
To ſhew thou loveſt me as thy ſiſters doe,
Accept a hufband, whom my felf will woo.
This faid, ſhe cannot well deny my fute,
Although (poore foule) her fences will be mute:

Then

Then will I triumph in my policy,
And match her with a king of *Brittany.*

Skalliger.

Ile to them before, and bewray your fecrecy.

Perillus.

Thus fathers think their children to beguile,
And oftentimes themfelves do firft repent,
When heavenly powers do fruftrate their intent.   [*Exeunt.*

Enter Gonorill *and* Ragan.

Gonorill.

I marvel, *Ragan,* how you can indure
To fee that proud pert peat, our youngeft fifter,
So flightly to account of us, her elders,
As if we were no better then her felf!
We cannot have a quaint device fo foone,
Or new made fafhion, of our choice invention;
But if fhe like it, fhe will have the fame,
Or ftudy newer to exceed us both.
Befides, fhe is fo nice and fo demure;
So fober, courteous, modeft, and precife,
That all the court hath work ynough to do,
To talke how fhe exceedeth me and you.

Ragan.

What fhould I do? would it were in my power,
To find a cure for this contagious ill:
Some defperate medicine muft be foone applied,
To dimme the glory of her mounting fame;
Els ere't be long, fheele have both prick and praife,
And we muft be fet by for working dayes.
Doe you not fee what feveral choice of futers
She daily hath, and of the beft degree?
Say, amongft all, fhe hap to fancy one,
And have a hufband when as we have none:
Why then, by right, to her we muft give place,
Though it be ne're fo much to our difgrace.

Gonorill.

By my virginity, rather then fhe fhall have
A hufband before me,
Ile marry one or other in his fhirt:

And

And yet I have made halfe a graunt already
Of my good will unto the king of *Cornwall*.

Ragan.

Sweare not fo deeply (fifter) here commeth my L. *Skalliger*.
Something his hafty comming doth import.

Enter Skalliger.

Skalliger.

Sweet princeffes, I am glad I met you heere fo luckily,
Having good newes which doth concerne you both,
And craveth fpeedy expedition.

Ragan.

For Gods fake tell us what it is, my lord,
I am with child untill you utter it.

Skalliger.

Madam, to fave your longing, this it is:
Your father in great fecrecy to day
Told me, he meanes to marry you out of hand
Unto the noble prince of *Cambria*;
You, madam, to the king of *Cornwalls* grace:
Your yonger fifter he would faine beftow
Upon the rich king of *Hibernia:*
But that he doubts, fhe hardly will confent;
For hitherto fhe ne're could fancy him.
If fhe do yeeld, why then, betweene you three,
He will devide his kingdome for your dowries.
But yet there is a further myftery,
Which, fo you will conceale, I will difclofe.

Gonorill.

What e'er thou fpeakft to us, kind *Skalliger*,
Thinke that thou fpeakft it only to thy felfe.

Skalliger.

He earneftly defireth for to know,
Which of you three do beare moft love to him,
And on your loves he fo extremely dotes,
As never any did, I thinke, before.
He prefently doth meane to fend for you,
To be refolv'd of this tormenting doubt:
And looke, whofe anfwere pleafeth him the beft,
They fhall have moft unto their marriages.

B b 4 *Ragan.*

Ragan.

O that I had fome pleafing mermaids voice,
For to inchaunt his fencelefle fences with!

Skalliger.

For he fuppofeth that *Cordella* will
(Striving to go beyond you in her love)
Promife to do what ever he defires :
Then will he ftraight enjoine her for his fake,
The *Hibernian* king in marriage for to take.
This is the fumme of all I have to fay;
Which being done, I humbly take my leave,
Not doubting but your wifdomes will forefee
What courfe will beft unto your good agree.

Gonorill.

Thanks, gentle *Skalliger*, thy kindnes undeferved,
Shall not be unrequited, if we live.   [*Exit* Skalliger.

Ragan.

Now have we fit occafion offred us,
To be reveng'd upon her unperceiv'd.

Gonorill.

Nay, our revenge we will inflict on her
Shall be accounted piety in us :
I will fo flatter with my doting father,
As he was ne're fo flattred in his life.
Nay, I will fay, that if it be his pleafure,
To match me to a begger, I will yeeld :
For why, I know what ever I do fay,
He meanes to match me with the *Cornwall* king.

Ragan.

Ile fay the like : for I am well affured,
What e're I fay to pleafe the old mans mind,
Who dotes, as if he were a child againe,
I fhall injoy the noble *Cambrian* prince :
Only, to feed his humour, will fuffice,
To fay, I am content with any one
Whom heele appoint me ; this will pleafe him more
Then e're *Appolloes* mufike pleafed *Jove.*

Gonorill.

I fmile to think, in what a wofull plight
Cordella will be, when we anfwere thus :

For ſhe will rather dye, then give conſent
To joine in marriage with the *Iriſh* king :
So will our father think, ſhe loveth him not,
Becauſe ſhe will not graunt to his deſire,
Which we will aggravate in ſuch bitter termes,
That he will ſoone convert his love to hate :
For he, you know, is alwayes in extremes.

Ragan.

Not all the world could lay a better plot,
I long till it be put in practice.   [*Exeunt.*

Enter Leir *and* Perillus.

Leir.

Perillus, go ſeeke my daughters,
Will them immediately come and ſpeak with me.

Perillus.

I will, my gracious lord.   [*Exit.*

Leir.

Oh, what a combat feeles my panting heart,
'Twixt childrens love, and care of common weale !
How deare my daughters are unto my ſoul,
None knowes, but he, that knowes my thoghts and ſecret deeds.
Ah, little do they know the deare regard,
Wherein I hold their future ſtate to come :
When they ſecurely ſleepe on beds of downe,
Theſe aged eyes do watch for their behalfe :
While they like wantons ſport in youthful toyes,
This throbbing heart is pearſt with dire annoyes.
As doth the ſun exceed the ſmalleſt ſtarre,
So much the fathers love exceeds the childs.
Yet my complaynts are cauſleſſe : for the world
Affords not children more conformable :
And yet, me thinks, my mind preſageth ſtill
I know not what ; and yet I feare ſome ill.

Enter Perillus, *with the three daughters.*

Well, here my daughters come : I have found out
. A preſent meanes to rid me of this doubt.

Gonorill.

Gonorill.

Our royal lord and father, in all duty,
We come to know the tenour of your will,
Why you fo haftily have fent for us.

Leir.

Deare *Gonorill*, kind *Ragan*, fweet *Cordella*,
Ye florifhing branches of a kingly ftocke,
Sprung from a tree that once did flourifh greene,
Whofe bloffomes now are nipt with winters froft,
And pale grym death doth wayt upon my fteps,
And fummons me unto his next affizes.
Therefore, deare daughters, as ye tender the fafety
Of him that was the caufe of your firft being,
Refolve a doubt which much molefts my mind,
Which of you three to me would prove moft kind;
Which loves me moft, and which at my requeft
Will fooneft yeeld unto their fathers heft.

Gonorill

I hope, my gracious father makes no doubt
Of any of his daughters love to him:
Yet for my part, to fhew my zeal to you,
Which cannot be in windy words rehearft,
I prize my love to you at fuch a rate,
I thinke my life inferiour to my love.
Should you injoine me for to tie a milftone
About my neck, and leape into the fea,
At your commaund I willingly would doe it:
Yea, for to doe you good, I would afcend
The higheft turret in all *Brittany*,
And from the top leape headlong to the ground:
Nay, more, fhould you appoint me for to marry
The meaneft vaffaile in the fpacious world,
Without reply I would accomplifh it:
In briefe, commaund whatever you defire,
And if I faile, no favour I require.

Leir.

O, how thy words revive my dying foule!

Cordella.

O, how I doe abhorre this flattery!

2   *Leir.*

Leir.

But what fayth *Ragan* to her father's will?　•

Ragan.

O, that my fimple utterance could fuffice,
To tell the true intention of my heart,
Which burnes in zeale of duty to your grace,
And never can be quench'd, but by defire
To fhew the fame in outward forwardneffe.
Oh, that there were fome other maid that durft
But make a challenge of her love with me;
Ide make her foone confeffe fhe never loved
Her father halfe fo well as I doe you.
I then my deeds fhould prove in plainer cafe,
How much my zeale aboundeth to your grace:
But for them all, let this one meane fuffice.
To ratify my love before your eyes:
I have right noble futers to my love,
No worfe then kings, and happely I love one:
Yes, would you have me make my choice anew,
Ide bridle fancy, and be rulde by you.

Leir.

Did never *Philomel* fing fo fweet a note.

Cordella.

Did never flatterer tell fo falfe a tale.

Leir.

Speak now, *Cordella*, make my joyes at full,
And drop downe nectar from thy hony lips.

Cordella.

I cannot paint my duty forth in words,
I hope my deeds fhall make report for me:
But looke what love the child doth owe the father,
The fame to you I beare, my gracious lord.

Gonorill.

Here is an anfwere anfwerleffe indeed:
Were you my daughter, I fhould fcarcely brooke it.

Ragan.

Doft thou not blufh, proud peacock as thou art,
To make our father fuch a flight reply?

Leir.

Leir.

Why how now, minion, are you growne fo proud ?
Doth our deare love make you thus peremptory ?
What, is your love become fo fmall to us,
As that you fcorne to tell us what it is ?
Do you love us, as every child doth love
Their father ? True indeed, as fome,
Who by difobedience fhort their fathers dayes,
And fo would you ; fome are fo father-fick,
That they make meanes to rid them from the world ;
And fo would you : fome are indifferent,
Whether their aged parents live or die ;
And fo are you. But, didft thou know, proud girle,
What care I had to fofter thee to this,
Ah, then thou wouldft fay as thy fifters do :
Our life is leffe, then love we owe to you.

Cordella.

Deare father, do not fo miftake my words,
Nor my plaine meaning be mifconftrued ;
My toung was never ufde to flattery.

Gonorill.

You were not beft fay I flatter : if you do,
My deeds fhall fhew, I flatter not with you.
I love my father better then thou canft.

Cordella.

The praife were great, fpoke from another's mouth :
But it fhould feeme your neighbours dwell far off.

Ragan.

Nay, here is one, that will confirme as much
As fhe hath faid, both for myfelfe and her.
I fay, thou doft not with my father's good.

Cordella.

Deare father——

Leir.

Peace, baftard impe, no iffue of king *Leir*,
I will not heare thee fpeake one tittle more.
Call not me father, if thou love thy life,
Nor thefe thy fifters once prefume to name :
Looke for no helpe henceforth from me or mine ;
Shift as thou wilt, and truft unto thyfelfe :

My

My kingdome will I equally devide
'Twixt thy two fisters to their royal dowre,
And will beftow them worthy their deferts :
This done, becaufe thou fhalt not have the hope
To have a child's part in the time to come,
I prefently will difpoffeffe myfelfe,
And fet up thefe vpon my princely throne.

Gonorill.

I ever thought that pride would have a fall.

Ragan.

Plaine dealing, fifter : your beauty is fo fheene,
You need no dowry, to make you be a queene.

[*Exeunt* Leir, Gonorill, Ragan.

Cordella.

Now whither, poore forfaken, fhall I goe,
When mine owne fifters tryumph in my woe?
But unto him which doth protect the juft,
In him will poore *Cordella* put her truft.
Thefe hands fhall labour, for to get my fpending ;
And fo Ile live until my days have ending.

Perillus.

Oh, how I grieve, to fee my lord thus fond,
To dote fo much upon vaine flattering words.
Ah, if he but with good advice had weighed,
The hidden tenure of her humble fpeech,
Reafon to rage fhould not have given place,
Nor poore *Cordella* fuffer fuch difgrace.   [*Exit.*

Enter the Gallian *king with* Mumford, *and three nobles more.*

King.

Diffwade me not, my lords, I am refolv'd,
This next faire wind to faile for *Brittany,*
In fome difguife, to fee if flying fame
Be not too prodigal in the wondrous praife
Of thefe three nymphes, the daughters of king *Leir.*
If prefent view do anfwere abfent praife,
And eyes allow of what our ears have heard,
And *Venus* ftand aufpicious to my vowes,
And fortune favour what I take in hand ;

I will

I will returne feiz'd of as rich a prize
As *Iafon*, when he wanne the golden fleece.

Mumford.

Heavens graunt you may : the match were ful of honor,
And well befeeming the young *Gallian* king.
I would your grace would favour me fo much,
As make me partner of your pilgrimage.
I long to fee the gallant *Britifh* dames,
And feed mine eyes upon their rare perfections :
For till I know the contrary, Ile fay,
Our dames in *Fraunce* are far more faire then they.

King.

Lord *Mumford,* you have faved me a labour,
In offring that which I did meane to afke :
And I moft willingly accept your company.
Yet firft I will injoine you to obferve
Some few conditions which I fhall propofe.

Mumford.

So that you do not tye mine eyes for looking
After the amorous glaunces of faire dames :
So that you do not tye my tong from fpeaking,
My lips from kiffing, when occafion ferves,
My hands from congees, and my knees to bow
To gallant girles; which were a tafke more hard,
Then flefh and bloud is able to indure :
Commaund what elfe you pleafe, I reft content.

King.

To bind thee from a thing thou canft not leave,
Were but a meane to make thee feeke it more :
And therefore fpeake, looke, kiffe, falute for me ;
In thefe myfelfe am like to fecond thee.
Now heare thy tafke. I charge thee from the time
That firft we fet faile for the *Brittifh* fhore,
To ufe no words of dignity to me,
But in the friendlieft manner that thou canft,
Make ufe of me as thy companion :
For we will go difguifde in palmers weeds,
That no man fhall miftruft us what we are.

Mumford.

Mumford.

If that be all, Ile fit your turne I warrant you. I am fome
kin to the *Blunts*, and, I think, the blunteft of all my kindred;
therefore if I bee too blunt with you, thanke yourfelfe for
praying me to be fo.

King.

Thy pleafant company will make the way feeme fhort.
It refteth now, that in my abfence hence,
I do commit the government to you
My trufty lords and faithful counfellers.
Time cutteth off the reft I have to fay :
The wind blowes faire, and I muft n.eds away.

Nobles.

Heavens fend your voyage to as good effect,
As we your land do purpofe to protect.   [*Exeunt.*

Enter the king of Cornwall *and his man booted and fpurd, a
riding wand, and a letter in his hand.*

Cornwall.

But how far diftant are we from the court ?

Servant.

Some twenty miles, my lord, or thereabouts.

Cornwall.

It feemeth to me twenty thoufand miles :
Yet hope I to be there within this houre.   [*To himfelfe.*

Servant.

Then are you like to ride alone for me.
I thinke my lord is weary of his life.

Cornwall.

Sweet *Gonorill*, I long to fee thy face,
Which haft fo kindly gratified my love.

Enter the king of Cambria *booted and fpurd, and his man with
a wand and a letter.*

Cambria.

Get a frefh horfe : for by my foule I fweare,
                                     [*He lookes on the letter.*
I am paft patience, longer to forbeare

                                                          The

The wifhed fight of my beloved miftris,
Deare *Ragan*, ftay and comfort of my life.
Servant.
Now what in God's name doth my lord intend?

[*To himfelfe.*

He thinks he ne'er fhall come at's journey's end.
I would he had old *Dedalus* waxen wings,
That he might flye, fo I might ftay behind:
For ere we get to *Troynovant*, I fee,
He quite will tire himfelfe, his horfe, and me.

Cornwall **and** *Cambria* looke one upon another, and ftart to fee eche other there.

Cornwall.
Brother of *Cambria*, we greet you well,
As one whom here we little did expect.
Cambria.
Brother of *Cornwall*, met in happy time:
I thought as much to have met with the fouldan of *Perfia*,
As to have met you in this place, my lord.
No doubt, it is about fome great affaires,
That makes you here fo flenderly accompanied.
Cornwall.
To fay the truth, my lord, it is no leffe,
And for your part fome hafty wind of chance
Hath blowne you hither thus upon the fudden.
Cambria.
My lord, to break off further circumftances,
For at this time I cannot brooke delayes:
Tell you your reafon, I will tell you mine.
Cornwall.
In faith content, and therefore to be briefe;
For I am fure my hafte's as great af yours:
I am fent for, to come unto king *Leir*,
Who by thefe prefent letters promifeth
His eldeft daughter, lovely *Gonorill*,
To me in mariage, and for prefent dowry,
The moity of halfe his regiment.

I   The

The ladies love I long ago poffeft :
But until now I never had the fathers.

Cambria.

You tell me wonders, yet I will relate
Strange newes, and henceforth we muft brothers call;   ×
Witneffe thefe lines : his honourable age,
Being weary of the troubles of his crowne,
His princely daughter *Ragan* will beftow
On me in mariage, with halfe his feigniories,
Whom I would gladly have accepted of,
With the third part, her complements are fuch.

Cornwall.

If I have one halfe, and you have the other,
Then betweene us we muft needs have the whole.

Cambria.

The hole ! how meane you that ? zlood, I hope,
We fhall have two holes betweene us.

Cornwall.

Why, the whole kingdome.

Cambria.

I, that's very true.

Cornwall.

What then is left for his third daughters dowry,
Lovely *Cordella,* whom the world admires ?

Cambria.

'Tis very ftrange, I know not what to thinke,
Unleffe they meane to make a nunne of her.

Cornwall.

'Twere pity fuch rare beauty fhould be hid
Within the compaffe of a cloyfters wall :
But howfoe'er, if *Leir's* words prove true,
It will be good, my lord, for me and you.

Cambria.

Then let us hafte, all danger to prevent,
For feare delayes doe alter his intent.   [*Exeunt.*

Enter Gonorill *and* Regan.

Gonorill.

Sifter, when did you fee *Cordella* laft,
That pretty piece, that thinks none good ynough

To

To ſpeake to her, becauſe (ſir-reverence)
She hath a little beauty extraordinary ?

Ragan.

Since time my father warnd her from his preſence,
I never ſaw her, that I can remember.
God give her joy of her ſurpaſſing beauty ;
I thinke, her dowry will be ſmall ynough.

Gonorill.

I have inceuſt my father ſo againſt her,
As he will never be reclaimd againe.

Ragan.

I was not much behind to do the like.

Gonorill.

Faith, ſiſter, what moves you to beare her ſuch good will ?

Ragan.

In truth, I thinke, the ſame that moveth you ;
Becauſe ſhe doth ſurpaſſe us both in beauty.

Gonorill.

Beſhrew your fingers, how right you can geſſe :
I tell you true, it cuts me to the heart.

Ragan.

But we will keepe her low enough, I warrant,
And clip her wings for mounting up too hie.

Gonorill.

Who ever hath her, ſhall have a rich mariage of her.

Ragan.

She were right fit to make a parſon's wife :
For they, men ſay, do love faire women well,
And many times doe marry them with nothing.

Gonorill.

With nothing ! marry God forbid : why, are there any ſuch ?

Ragan.

I mean, no money.

Gonorill.

I cry you mercy, I miſtooke you much :
And ſhe is far too ſtately for the church ;
Sheele lay her huſband's benefice on her back,
Even in one gowne, if ſhe may have her will.

Ragan.

In faith, poore ſoul, I pitty her a little.
Would ſhe were leſſe faire, or more fortunate.

Well,

Well, I thinke long untill I fee my *Morgan*,   x
The gallant prince of *Cambria*, here arrive.
                    Gonorill.
  And fo do I, until the *Cornwall* king
Prefent himfelfe, to confummate my joyes.
Peace, here commeth my father.

        Enter Leir, Perillus, *and others.*

                Leir.
  Ceafe, good my lords, and fue not to reverfe
Our cenfure, which is now irrevocable,
We have difpatched letters of contract
Unto the kings of *Cambria* and of *Cornwall*;
Our hand and feale will juftify no leffe:
Then do not fo difhonour me, my lords,
As to make fhipwrack of our kingly word.
I am as kind as is the pellican,
That kils it felfe, to fave her young ones lives:
And yet as jelous as the princely eagle,
That kils her young ones, if they do but dazell
Upon the radiant fplendor of the funne.
Within this two dayes I expect their coming.

        Enter kings of Cornwall *and* Cambria.

But in good time, they are arriv'd already.
This hafte of yours, my lords, doth teftify
The fervent love you beare unto my daughters:
And think your felves as welcome to king *Leir,*
As ever *Pryams* children were to him.
                Cornwall.
  My gracious lord, and father too, I hope,
Pardon, for that I made no greater hafte:
But were my horfe as fwift as was my will,
I long ere this had feene your majefty.
                Cambria.
  No other fcufe of abfence can I frame,
Then what my brother hath inform'd your grace:
For our undeferved welcome, we do vowe,
Perpetually to reft at your commaund.
            C c 2   *Cornwall.*

Cornwall.

But you, fweet love, illuftrious *Gonorill*,
The regent, and the foveraigne of my foule,
Is *Cornwall* welcome to your excellency?

Gonorill.

As welcome, as *Leander* was to *Hero*,
Or brave *Aeneas* to the *Carthage* queene:
So and more welcome is your grace to me.

Cambria.

O, may my fortune prove no worfe then his,
Since heavens do know, my fancy is as much.
Deare *Ragan*, fay, if welcome unto thee,
All welcomes elfe will little comfort me.

Ragan.

As gold is welcome to the covetous eye,
As fleepe is welcome to the traveller,
As is frefh water to fea-beaten men,
Or moiftned fhowres unto the parched ground,
Or any thing more welcomer then this,
So and more welcome lovely *Morgan* is.

Leir.

What refteth then, but that we confummate
The celebration of thefe nuptiall rites?
My kingdome I do equally devide.
Princes, draw lots, and take your chaunce as falles.

[*Then they draw lots.*

Thefe I refigne as freely unto you,
As earft by true fucceffion they were mine.
And here I do freely difpoffeffe my felfe,
And make you two my true adopted heires:
My felfe will fojorne with my fonne of *Cornwall*,
And take me to my prayers and my beades.
I know, my daughter *Ragan* will be forry,
Becaufe I do not fpend my dayes with her:
Would I were able to be with both at once;
They are the kindeft girles in *Chriftendome*.

Perillus.

I have bin filent all this while, my lord,
To fee if any worthier then my felfe,
Would once have fpoke in poore *Cordellaes* caufe:

4   But

But love or feare ties filence to their toungs.
Oh, heare me fpeake for her, my gracious lord,
Whofe deeds have not deferv'd this ruthlefle doome,
As thus to difinherit her of all.

Leir.

Urge this no more, and if thou love thy life:
I fay, fhe is no daughter, that doth fcorne
To tell her father how fhe loveth him.
Who ever fpeaketh hereof to mee againe,
I will efteeme him for my mortal foe.
Come, let us in, to celebrate with joy,
The happy nuptialls of thefe lovely paires.

[*Exeunt omnes, manet* Perillus.

Perillus.

Ah, who fo blind, as they that will not fee
The neere approch of their owne mifery?
Poore lady, I extremely pitty her :
And whileft I live, eche drop of my heart blood
Will I ftraine forth, to do her any good.　　　　[*Exit.*

Enter the Gallian *king, and* Mumford, *difguifed like pilgrims.*

Mumford.

My lord, how do you brook this *Brittifh* aire?

King.

My lord, I told you of this foolifh humour,
And bound you to the contrary, you know.

Mumford.

Pardon me for once, my lord ; I did forget.

King.

My lord againe? then let's have nothing elfe,
And fo be tane for fpies, and then tis well.

Mumford.

Swounds, I could bite my toung in two for anger :
For Gods fake name yourfelf fome proper name.

King.

Call me *Trefillus:* Ile call thee *Denapoll.*

Mumford.

Might I be made the monarch of the world,
I could not hit upon thefe names, I fweare.

C c 3

King.

King.

Then call me *Will,* Ile call thee *Jacke.*

Mumford.

Well, be it fo, for I have weil deferv'd to be cal'd *Jack.*

King.

Stand clofe; for here a *Brittifh* lady commeth:

Enter Cordella.

A fairer creature ne're mine eyes beheld.

Cordella.

This is a day of joy unto my fifters,
Wherein they both are maried unto kings;
And I, by birth, as werthy as themfelves,
Am ternd into the world, to feeke my fortune.
How may I blame the fickle queene of chaunce,
That maketh me a patterne of her power?
Ah, poore weake maid, whofe imbecility
Is far unable to indure thefe brunts.
Oh, father *Leir,* how doft thou wrong thy child,
Who alwayes was obedient to thy will!
But why accufe I fortune and my father?
No, no, it is the pleafure of my God:
And I do willingly imbrace the rod.

King.

It is no goddeffe; for fhe doth complaine
On fortune, and th' unkindneffe of her father.

Cordella.

Thefe coftly robes ill fitting my eftate,
I will exchange for other meaner habit.

Mumford.

Now if I had a kingdome in my hands,
I would exchange it for a milkmaids fmock and peticoate,
That fhe and I might fhift our clothes together.

Cordella.

I will betake me to my thred and needle,
And earne my living with my fingers ends.

Mumford.

O brave! God willing, thou fhalt have my cuftome.
By fweet S. *Denis,* here I fadly fweare,
For all the fhirts and night-geare that I weare.

Cordella.

Cordella.

I will profeffe and vow a maidens life.

Mumford.

Then I proteft thou fhalt not have my cuftom.

King.

I can forbeare no longer for to fpeak :
For if I do, I think my heart will breake.

Mumford.

Sblood, *Wil*, I hope you are not in love with my fempfter.

King.

I am in fuch a laborinth of love,
As that I know not which way to get out.

Mumford.

You'l ne're get out, unlefie you firft get in.

King.

I prithy *Jacke*, croffe not my paffions.

Mumford.

Prithy *Wil*, to her, and try her patience.

King.

Thou faireft creature, whatfoere thou art,
That ever any mortal eyes beheld,
Vouchfafe to me, who have o'reheard thy woes,
To fhew the caufe of thefe thy fad laments.

Cordella.

Ah pilgrims, what availes to fhew the caufe,
When there's no meanes to find a remedy?

King.

To utter griefe, doth eafe a heart o'recharg'd.

Cordella.

To touch a fore, doth aggravate the paine.

King.

The filly moufe, by vertue of her teeth,
Releas'd the princely lion from the net.

Cordella.

Kind palmer, which fo much defir'ft to heare
The tragick tale of my unhappy youth :
Know this in briefe, I am the hapleffe daughter
Of *Leir*, fometimes king of *Brittany*.

King.

Why, who debarres his honourable age,
From being ftill the king of *Brittany?*

C c 4   *Cordella.*

Cordella.

None, but himfelfe hath difpoffeft himfelfe,
And given all his kingdome to the kings
Of *Cornwall* and of *Cambria*, with my fifters.

King.

Hath he given nothing to your lovely felfe?

Cordella.

He lov'd me not, and therefore gave me nothing,
Only becaufe I could not flatter him:
And in this day of triumph to my fifters,
Doth fortune triumph in my overthrow. . .

King.

Sweet lady, fay there fhould come a king,
As good as either of your fifters hufbands,
To crave your love, would you accept of him?

Cordella.

Oh, doe not mocke with thofe in mifery,
Nor do not think, though fortune have the power,
To fpoile mine honour, and debafe my ftate,
That fhe hath any intereft in my mind:
For if the greateft monarch on the earth,
Should fue to me in this extremity,
Except my heart could love, and heart could like,
Better then any that I ever faw,
His great eftate no more fhould move my mind,
Then mountaines move by blaft of every wind.

King.

Think not, fweet nymph, tis holy palmers guife,
To grieved foules frefh torments to devife:
Therefore in witneffe of my true intent,
Let heaven and earth beare record of my words:
There is a young and lufty *Gallian* king,
So like to me, as I am to myfelfe,
That earneftly doth crave to have thy love,
And joine with thee in *Hymens* facred bonds.

Cordella.

The like to thee did ne're thefe eyes behold;
Oh live to adde new torments to my griefe:
Why didft thou thus intrap me unawares?
Ah palmer, my eftate doth not befit

A kingly

A kingly mariage, as the cafe now ftands.
Whilome when as I liv'd in honours height,
A prince perhaps might poftulate my love:
Now mifery, difhonour, and difgrace,
Hath light on me, and quite reverft the cafe.
Thy king will hold thee wife, if thou furceafe
The fute, whereas no dowry will infue.
Then be advifed, palmer, what to do :
Ceafe for thy king, feeke for thy felfe to woo.

King.
Your birth's too high for any, but a king.

Cordella.
My mind is low ynough to love a palmer,
Rather then any king upon the earth.

King.
O, but you never can indure their life,
Which is fo ftraight and full of penury.

Cordella.
O yes, I can, and happy if I might :
Ile hold thy palmers ftaffe within my hand,
And thinke it is the fcepter of a queene.
Sometime Ile fet thy bonnet on my head,
And thinke I weare a rich imperial crowne.
Sometime Ile helpe thee in thy holy prayers,
And thinke I am with thee in paradife.
Thus Ile mock fortune, as fhe mocketh me,
And never will my lovely choice repent:
For, having thee, I fhall have all content.

King.
'Twere fin to hold her longer in fufpence,
Since that my foule hath vow'd fhe fhall be mine.
Ah, deare *Cordella*, cordial to my heart,
I am no palmer, as I feeme to be,
But hither come in this unkno vne difguife,
To view th' admired beauty of thofe eyes.
I am the king of *Gallia*, gentle maid,
(Although thus flenderly accompanied),
And yet thy vaffaile by imperious love,
And fworne to ferve thee everlaftingly.

Cordella.

What e're you be, of high or low difcent,
All's one to me, I do requeſt but this :
That as I am, you will accept of me,
And I will have you whatſoe're you be :
Yet well I know, you come of royal race,
I fee fuch fparks of honour in your face.

Mumford.

Have palmers weeds fuch power to win faire ladies ?
Faith, then I hope the next that falles is mine :
Upon condition I no worſe might ſpeed,
I would for ever weare a palmers weed.
I like an honeſt and plaine dealing wench,
That ſweares (without exceptions) I will have you.
Theſe foppets, that know not whether to love a man or no,
except they firſt go aſke their mothers leave, by this hand, I
hate them ten times worſe then poiſon.

King.

What refteth then our happineſſe to procure ?

Mumford.

Faith, go to church, to make the matter fure.

King.

It fhall be fo, becauſe the world fhall ſay,
King *Leirs* three daughters were wedded in one day :
The celebration of this happy chaunce,
We will deferre, until we come to *Fraunce*.

Mumford.

I like the wooing, that's not long a doing.
Well, for her fake, I know what I know :
Ile never marry whileſt I live,
Except I have one of theſe *Brittiſh* ladies,
My humour is alienated from the maids of *Fraunce*.   [*Exeunt.*

Enter Perillus *folus.*

Perillus.

The king hath difpoffeſt himſelfe of all,
Thofe to advaunce, which fcarce will give him thanks :
His youngeſt daughter he hath turnd away,
And no man knowes what is become of her.

He

He sojourns now in *Cornwall* with the eldest,
Who flattred him, until she did obtaine
That at his hands, which now she doth possesse :
And now she sees hee hath no more to give,
It grieves her heart to see her father live,
Oh, whom should man trust in this wicked age,
When children thus against their parents rage?
But he, the myrrour of mild patience,
Puts up all wrongs, and never gives reply :
Yet shames she not in most opprobrious sort,
To call him foole and doterd to his face,
And sets her parasites of purpose oft,
In scoffing wise to offer him difgrace.
Oh yron age! O times! O monstrous, vilde,
When parents are contemned of the child !
His penfion she hath halfe reftrain'd from him,
And will, ere long, the other halfe, I feare ;
For she thinks nothing is beftowde in vaine,
But that which doth her father's life maintaine.
Truft not alliance; but truft ftrangers rather,
Since daughters prove difloyal to the father.
Well, I wil counfel him the beft I can :
Would I were able to redreffe his wrong,
Yet what I can, unto my utmoft power,
He shall be sure of to the lateft houre.   [*Exit.*

Enter Gonorill *and* Skalliger.

Gonorill.

I prithy, *Skalliger*, tell me what thou thinkft :
Could any woman of our dignity
Endure fuch quips and peremptory taunts,
As I do daily from my doting father ?
Doth't not fuffice that I him keepe of almes,
Who is not able for to keepe himfelfe ?
But as if he were our better, he fhould thinke
To check and fnap me up at every word.
I cannot make me a new fafhioned gowne,
And fet it forth with more then common coft ;

But

But his old doting doltish withered wit,
Is sure to give a fencelesse check for it.
I cannot make a banquet extraordinary,
To grace myselfe, and spread my name abroad,
But he, old foole, is captious by and by,
And saith, the cost would well suffice for twice.
Judge then, I pray, what reason is't, that I
Should stand alone charg'd with his vaine expence,
And that my sister *Ragan* should go free,
To whom he gave as much, as unto me?
I prithy, *Skalliger*, tell me, if thou know,
By any meanes to rid me of this woe.

                    Skalliger.
Your many favours still bestowde on me,
Binde me in duty to advise your grace,
How you may soonest remedy this ill.
The large allowance which he hath from you,
Is that which makes him so forget himselfe:
Therefore abbridge it halfe, and you shall see,
That having lesse, he will more thankful be:
For why, abundance maketh us forget
The fountaines whence the benefits do spring.

                    Gonorill.
Well. *Skalliger*, for thy kind advice herein,
I will not be ungrateful, if I live:
I have restrained halfe his portion already,
And I will presently restraine the other,
That having no meanes to releeve himselfe,
He may go seeke elsewhere for better helpe.   [*Exit.*

                    Skalliger,
Go, viperous woman, shame to all thy sexe:
The heavens, no doubt, will punish thee for this:
And me a villaine, that to curry favour,
Have given the daughter counsel 'gainst the father.
But us the world doth this experience give,
That he that cannot flatter, cannot live.   [*Exit.*

                                        Enter

Enter king of Cornwall, Leir, Perillus, *and nobles.*

Cornwall.
Father, what aileth you to be fo fad ?
Methinks, you frollike not as you were wont.
Leir.
The neerer we do grow unto our graves,
The leffe we do delight in worldly joyes.
Cornwall.
But if a man can frame himfelfe to mirth,
It is a meane for to prolong his life.
Leir.
Then welcome forrow, *Leir's* only friend,
Who doth defire his troubled dayes had end.
Cornwall.
Comfort yourfelfe, father, here comes your daughter,
Who much will grieve, I know, to fee you fad.

Enter Gonorill.

Leir.
But more doth grieve, I feare, to fee me live.
Cornwall.
My *Gonorill,* you come in wifhed time,
To put your father from thefe penfive dumps.
In faith, I feare that all things go not well.
Gonorill.
What, do you feare, that I have angred him ?
Hath he complained of me unto my lord ?
Ile provide him a piece of bread and cheefe ;
For in a time heele practife nothing elfe,
Then carry tales from one unto another.
'Tis all his practife for to kindle ftrife,
'Twixt you, my lord, and me your loving wife :
But I will take an order, if I can,
To ceafe th'effect, where firft the caufe began.
Cornwall.
Sweet, be not angry in a partial caufe,
He ne'er complain'd of thee in all his life.
Father, you muft not weigh a woman's words.

Leir.

Leir.

Alas, not I : poore foule, fhe breeds yong bones,
And that is it makes her fo turchy fure.

Gonorill.

What, breeds young bones already! you will make
An honeft woman of me then, belike.
O vild olde wretch! who ever heard the like,
That feeketh thus his owne child to defame ?

Cornwall.

I cannot ftay to heare this difcord found.   [*Exit.*

Gonorill.

For any one that loves your company,
You may go pack, and feeke fome other place,
To fowe the feed of difcord and difgrace.   [*Exit.*

Leir.

Thus, fay or do the beft that e'er I can,
'Tis wrefted ftraight into another fence :
This punifhment my heavy finnes deferve,
And more then this ten thoufand thoufand times :
Elfe aged *Leir* them could never find
Cruel to him, to whom he hath bin kind.
Why do I over-live myfelfe, to fee
The courfe of nature quite reverft in me ?
Ah, gentle death, if ever any wight
Did wifh thy prefence with a perfit zcale :
Then come, I pray thee, even with all my heart,
And end my forrowes with thy fatal dart.   [*He weepes.*

Perillus.

Ah, do not fo difconfolate yourfelfe,
Nor dew your aged cheeks with wafting tears.

Leir.

What man art thou that takeft any pity
Upon the worthleffe ftate of old *Leir* ?

Perillus.

One, who doth beare as great a fhare of griefe,
As if it were my deareft father's cafe.

Leir.

Ah, good my friend, how ill art thou advifde,
For to confort with miferable men :

Go

Go learne to flatter, where thou mayſt in time
Get favour 'mongſt the mighty, and ſo clime:
For now I am ſo poore and full of want,
As that I ne're can recompence thy love.

Perillus.

What's got by flattery, doth not long indure;
And men in favour live not moſt ſecure.
My conſcience tels me, if I ſhould forſake you,
I were the hatefulſt excrement on the earth:
Which well do know, in courſe of former time,
How good my lord hath bin to me and mine.

Leir.

Did I ere raiſe thee higher then the reſt
Of all thy anceſtors which were before?

Perillus.

I ne're did ſeeke it; but by your good grace,
I ſtill injoyed my owne with quietneſſe.

Leir.

Did I ere give thee living, to increaſe
The due revenues which thy father left?

Perillus.

I had ynough, my lord, and having that,
What ſhould you need to give me any more?

Leir.

Oh, did I ever diſpoſſeſſe my ſelfe,
And give thee halfe my kingdome in good will?

Perillus.

Alas, my lord, there were no reaſon, why
You ſhould have ſuch a thought, to give it me.

Leir.

Nay, if thou talke of reaſon, then be mute;
For with good reaſon I can thee confute.
If they, which firſt by natures ſacred law
Do owe to me the tribute of their lives;
If they to whom I alwayes have bin kinde,
And bountiful beyond compariſon;
If they, for whom I have undone my ſelfe,
And brought my age unto this extreme want,
Do now reject, contemne, deſpiſe, abhor me,
What reaſon moveth thee to ſorrow for me?

3

Perillus.

Perillus.

Where reafon failes, let teares confirme my love,
And fpeake how much your paffions do me move.
Ah, good my lord, condemne not all for one:
You have two daughters left, to whom I know
You fhall be welcome, if you pleafe to go.

Leir.

Oh, how thy words adde forrow to my foule,
To thinke of my unkindneffe to *Cordella!*
Whom caufeleffe I did difpoffeffe of all.
Upon th' unkind fuggeftions of her fifters:
And for her fake, I thinke this heavy doome
Is falne on me, and not without defert:
Yet unto *Ragan* was I alwayes kinde,
And gave to her the halfe of all I had:
It may be, if,I fhould to her repaire,
She would be kinder, and intreat me faire.

Perillus.

No doubt fhe would, and practife ere't be long,
By force of armes for to redreffe your wrong.

Leir.

Well, fince thou doeft advife me for to go,
I am refolv'd to try the worft of wo.   [*Exeunt.*

Enter Ragan *folus.*

Ragan.

How may I bleffe the howre of my nativity,
Which bodeth unto me fuch happy ftarres!
How may I thank kind fortune, that vouchfafes
To all my actions, fuch defir'd event!
I rule the king of *Cambria* as I pleafe:
The ftates are all obedient to my will;
And looke what ere I fay, it fhall be fo;
Not any one, that dareth anfwere no.
My eldeft fifter lives in royal ftate,
And wanteth nothing fitting her degree:
Yet hath fhe fuch a cooling card withall,
As that her hony favoureth much of gall.

My

My father with her is quarter-mafter ftill,
And many times reftraines her of her will:
But if he were with me, and ferv'd me fo,
Ide fend him packing fome where elfe to go.
Ide entertaine him with fuch flender coft,
That he fhould quickly wifh to change his hoft.　　　[*Exit.*

Enter Cornwall, Gonorill, *and attendants.*

Cornwall.

Ah, *Gonorill,* what dire unhappy chaunce
Hath fequeftred thy father from our prefence,
That no report can yet be heard of him?
Some great unkindneffe hath bin offred him,
Exceeding far the bounds of patience:
Elfe all the world fhall never me perfwade,
He would forfake us without notice made.

Gonorill.

Alas, my lord, whom doth it touch fo neere,
Or who hath intereft in this griefe, but I,
Whom forrow had brought to her longeft home,
But that I know his qualities fo well?
I know, he is but ftolne upon my fifter
At unawares, to fee her how fhe fares,
And fpend a little time with her, to note
How all things goe, and how fhe likes her choice:
And when occafion ferves, heele fteale from her,
And unawares returne to us againe.
Therefore, my lord, be frolick, and refolve
To fee my father here againe ere long.

Cornwall.

I hope fo too; but yet to be more fure,
Ile fend a pofte immediately to know
Whether he be arrived there or no.　　　[*Exit.*

Gonorill.

But I will intercept the meffenger,
And temper him before he doth depart
With fweet perfwafions, and with found rewards,
That his report fhall ratify my fpeech,
And make my lord ceafe further to inquire.
If he be not gone to my fifters court,

D d　　　　　　　　　　　　As

As fure my mind perfageth that he is,
He happely may, by travelling unknowne wayes,
Fall ficke, and as a common paffenger,
Be dead and buried : would God it were fo well;
For then there were no more to do, but this,
He went away, and none knowes where he is.
But fay he be in *Cambria* with the king,
And there exclaime againft me, as he will:
I know he is as welcome to my fifter,
As water is into a broken fhip.
Well, after him Ile fend fuch thunderclaps
Of flaunder, fcandal, and invented tales,
That all the blame fhall be remov'd from me,
And unperceiv'd rebound upon himfelfe.
Thus with one naile another Ile expel,
And make the world judge, that I ufde him well.

Enter the meffenger that fhould go to Cambria, *with a letter io
his hand.*

Gonorill.
My honeft friend, whither away fo faft ?
Meffenger.
To *Cambria*, madam, with letters from the king.
Gonorill.
To whom ?
Meffenger.
Unto your father, if he be there.
Gonorill.
Let me fee them.   [*She opens them.*
Meffenger.
Madam, I hope your grace will ftand
Betweene me and my neck-verfe, if I be
Call'd in queftion, for opening the king's letters.
Gonorill.
'Twas I that opened them, it was not thou.
Meffenger.
I, but you need not care ; and fo muft I,
A handfome man, be quickly truft up,
And when a man's hang'd, all the world cannot fave him.
Gonorill.

Gonorill.

He that hangs thee, were better hang his father,
Or that but hurts thee in the leaſt degree,
I tell thee, we make great account of thee.

Meſſenger.

I am o'er-joy'd, I ſurfet of ſweet words:
Kind queene, had I a hundred lives, I would
Spend ninety-nine of them for you, for that word.

Gonorill.

I, but thou wouldſt keepe one life ſtill,
And that's as many as thou art like to have.

Meſſenger.

That one life is not too deare for my good queene; this
ſword, this buckler, this head, this heart, theſe hands, armes,
legs, tripes, bowels, and all the members elſe whatſoever, are
at your diſpoſe; uſe me, truſt me, commaund me: if I faile in
any thing, tie me to a dung cart, and make a ſcavengers horſe
of me, and whip me ſo long as I have any ſkin on my back.

Gonorill.

In token of further imployment, take that.

                         [Flings him a purſe.

Meſſenger.

A ſtrong bond, a firme obligation, good in law, good in law:
if I keepe not the condition, let my necke be the forfeiture of
my negligence.

Gonorill.

I like thee well, thou haſt a good toung.

Meſſenger.

And as bad a toung, if it be ſet on it, as any oyſterwife at
Billinſgate hath: why, I have made many of my neighbours   ×
forſake their houſes with railing upon them, and go dwell elſe
where; and ſo by my meanes houſes have bin good cheape
in our pariſh: my toung being well whetted with choller,
is more ſharpe then a razer of *Palerno.*

Gonorill.

O thou art a fit man for my purpoſe.

Meſſenger.

Commend me not, ſweet queene, before you try me.
As my deſerts are, ſo do think of me.

                            Gonorill.

Gonorill.

Well faid, then this is thy trial: inftead of carrying the
king's letters to my father, carry thou thefe letters to my fifter,
which containe matter quite contrary to the other: there fhall
fhe be given to underftand, that my father hath detracted her,
given out flaundrous fpeaches againft her; and that hee hath
moft intollerably abufed me, fet my lord and me at variance,
and made mutinies amongft the commons.
Thefe things (although it be not fo)
Yet thou muft affirme them to be true,
With othes and proteftations as will ferve
To drive my fifter out of love with him,
And caufe my will accomplifhed to be.
This do, thou winft my favour for ever,
And makeft a hye way of preferment to thee
And all thy friends.

Meffenger.

It fufficeth, conceit it is already done :
I will fo toung-whip him, that I will
Leave him as bare of credit, as a poulter
Leaves a cony, when fhe pulls off his fkin.

Gonorill.

Yet there is a further matter.

Meffenger.

I thirft to heare it.

Gonorill.

If my fifter thinketh convenient, as my letters importeth, to
make him away, haft thou the heart to effect it?

Meffenger.

Few words are beft in fo fmall a matter :
Thefe are but trifles. By this booke I will. [*Kiffes the paper.*

Gonorill.

About it prefently, I long till it be done.

Meffenger.

I fly, I fly.   [*Exeunt.*

Enter Cordella *folus.*

Cordella.

I have bin over-negligent to day,
In going to the temple of my God,

To

To render thanks for all his benefits,
Which he miraculoufly hath beftowed on me,
In raifing me out of my meane eftate,
When as I was devoid of worldly friends,
And placing me in fuch a fweet content,
As far exceeds the reach of my deferts.
My kingly hufband, myrrour of his time,
For zeale, for juftice, kindneffe, and for care
To God, his fubjects, me, and common weale,
By his appointment was ordained for me.
I cannot wifh the thing that I do want ;
I cannot want the thing but I may have,
Save only this which I fhall ne're obtaine,
My father's love, oh this I ne're fhall gaine.
I would abftaine from any nutryment,
And pine my body to the very bones :
Bare foote I would on pilgrimage fet forth
Unto the furtheft quarters of the earth,
And all my life-time would I fackcloth weare,
And mourning-wife powre duft upon my head :
So he but to forgive me once would pleafe,
That his gray haires might go to heaven in peace.
And yet I know not how I him offended,
Or wherein juftly I have deferved blame.
Oh, fifters ! you are much to blame in this,
It was not he, but you that did me wrong :
Yet God forgive both him, and you, and me ;
Even as I doe in perfit charity.
I will to church, and pray unto my Saviour,
That ere I die, I may obtaine his favour.   [*Exit.*

Enter Leir *and* Perillus *faintly*.

Perillus.
Reft on me, my lord, and ftay yourfelfe,
The way feemes tedious to your aged limmes.
Leir.
Nay, reft on me, kind friend, and ftay thyfelfe,
Thou art as old as I, but more kind.

D d 3   Perillus.

Perillus.

Ah, good my lord, it ill befits, that I
Should leane upon the person of a king.

Leir.

But it fits worfe, that I fhould bring thee forth,
That had no caufe to come along with me,
Through thefe untouth paths, and tireful wayes,
And never eafe thy fainting limmes a whit.
Thou haft left all, I, all to come with me,
And I, for all, have nought to guerdon thee.

Perillus.

Ceafe, good my lord, to aggravate my woes
With thefe kind words, which cuts my heart in two,
To think your will fhould want the power to do.

Leir.

Ceafe, good *Perillus*, for to call me lord,
And think me but the fhaddow of myfelfe.

Perillus.

That honourable title will I give
Unto my lord, fo long as I do live.
Oh, be of comfort; for I fee the place
Whereas your daughter keeps her refidence.
And loe, in happy time the *Cambrian* prince
Is here arriv'd, to gratify our comming.

Enter the prince of Cambria, Ragan, *and nobles : looke upon them,
and whifper together.*

Leir,

Were I beft fpeak, or fit me downe and dye ?
I am afham'd to tell this heavy tale.

Perillus,

Then let me tell it, if you pleafe, my lord :
'Tis fhame for them that were the caufe thereof.

Cambria,

What two old men are thofe that feeme fo fad ?
Me thinks, I fhould remember well their lookes.

Ragan.

No, I miftake not, fure it is my father :
I muft diffemble kindneffe now of force,

She runneth to him, and kneeles downe, saying:

Father, I bid you welcome, full of griefe,
To see your grace ufde thus unworthily,
And ill befitting for your reverend age,
To come on foot a journey fo indurable.
Oh, what difafter chaunce hath bin the caufe,
To make your cheeks fo hollow, fpare and leane?
He cannot fpeake for weeping : for God's love, come,
Let us refrefh him with fome needful things,
And at more leifure we may better know,
Whence fprings the ground of this unlookt-for wo.
                              Cambria.
Come, father, ere we any further talke,
You fhall refrefh you after this weary walk.
                    [*Exeunt, manet* Ragan.
              Ragan.
Comes he to me with finger in the eye,
To tell a tale againft my fifter here?
Whom I do know, he greatly hath abufde :
And now like a contentious crafty wretch,
He firft begins for to complaine himfelfe,
When as himfelfe is in the greateft fault ?
Ile not be partial in my fifter's caufe,
Not yet beleeve his doting vaine reports :
Who for a trifle (fafely) I dare fay,
Upon a fpleene is ftolen thence away :
And here (forfooth) he hopeth to have harbour,
And to be moan'd and made on like a child :
But ere't be long, his comming he fhall curfe,
And truely fay, he came from bad to worfe :
Yet will I make faire weather, to procure
Convenient meanes, and then Ile ftrike it fure.   [*Exit.*

              Enter Meffenger folus.

                  Meffenger.
Now happily I am arrived here,
Before the ftately palace of the *Cambrian* king :
If *Leir* be here fafe-feated, and in reft,
To rowfe him from it I will do my beft.
              D d 4   *Enter*

Enter Ragan.

Now bags of gold, your vertue is (no doubt)
To make me in my meſſage bold and ſtout.
The King of heaven preſerve your majeſty,
And ſend your highneſſe everlaſting raigne.

Ragan.

Thanks, good my friend ; but what imports thy meſſage ?

Meſſenger.

Kind greetings from the *Cornwall* queene :
The reſidue theſe letters will declare.   [*She opens the letters.*

Ragan.

How fares our royal ſiſter ?

Meſſenger.

I did leave her, at my parting, in good health.
        [*She reads the letter, frownes, and ſtamps.*
See how her colour comes and goes againe,
Now red as ſcarlet, now as pale as aſh :
See how ſhe knits her brow, and bites her lips,
And ſtamps, and makes a dumbe ſhew of diſdaine,
Mixt with revenge, and violent extreames.
Here will be more worke and more crownes for me.

Ragan.

Alas, poore ſoule, and hath he uſde her thus ?
And is he now come hither, with intent
To ſet divorce betwixt my lord and me ?
Doth he give out, that he doth heare report,
That I do rule my huſband as I liſt,
And therefore meanes to alter ſo the caſe,
That I ſhall know my lord to be my head ?
Well, it were beſt for him to take good heed,
Or I will make him hop without a head,
For his preſumption, dottard that he is.
In *Cornwall* he hath made ſuch mutinies,
Firſt, ſetting of the king againſt the queene ;
Then ſtirring up the commons 'gainſt the king ;
That had he there continued any longer,
He had bin call'd in queſtion for his fact.
So upon that occaſion thence he fled,
And comes thus ſlily ſtealing unto us :

And·

And now already fince his coming hither,
My lord and he are growne in fuch a league,
That I can have no conference with his grace:
I feare, he doth already intimate
Some forged cavillations 'gainft my ftate: •
'Tis therefore beft to cut him off in time,
Left flaundcrous rumours once abroad difperft,
It is too late for them to be reverft.
Friend, as the tennour of thefe letters fhewes,
My fifter puts great confidence in thee.

Meffenger.

She never yet committed truft to me,
But that (I hope) fhe found me alwayes faithful:
So will I be to any friend of hers,
That hath occafion to imploy my helpe.

Ragan.

Haft thou the heart to act a ftratagem,
And give a ftabbe or two, if need require:

Meffenger.

I have a heart compact of adamant,
Which never knew what melting pitty meant.
I weigh no more the murdring of a man,
Then I refpect the cracking of a flea,
When I doe catch her biting on my fkin.
If you will have your hufband or your father,
Or both of them fent to another world,
Do but commaund me doo't, it fhall be done.

Ragan.

It is ynough, we make no doubt of thee:
Meet us to morrow here, at nine a clock:
Meane while, farewel, and drink that for my fake.   [Exit.

Meffenger.

I, this is it will make me do the deed:
Oh, had I every day fuch cuftomers,
This were the gainefulft trade in Chriftendome!
A purfe of gold giv'n for a paltry ftabbe!
Why, heres a wench that longs to have a ftabbe.
Wel, I could give it her, and ne're hurt her neither.

Enter

Enter the Gallian *king,* *and* Cordella.

King.

When will thefe clouds of forrow once difperfe,
And fmiling joy triumph upon thy brow?
When will this fcene of fadneffe have an end,
And pleafant acts infue, to move delight?
When will my lovely queene ceafe to lament,
And take fome comfort to her grieved thoughts?
If of thyfelfe thou daignft to have no care,
Yet pitty me, whom thy griefe makes defpaire.

Cordella.

O, grieve not you, my lord, you have no caufe;
Let not my paffions move your mind a whit:
For I am bound by nature to lament
For his ill will, that life to me firft lent.
If fo the ftocke be dryed with difdaine,
Withered and fere the branch muft needs remaine.

King.

But thou art now graft in another ftock;
I am the ftock, and thou the lovely branch:
And from my root continual fap fhall flow,
To make thee flourifh with perpetual fpring.
Forget thy father and thy kindred now,
Since they forfake thee like inhumane beaftes;
Thinke they are dead, fince all their kindneffe dies,
And bury them, where black oblivion lies.
Think not thou art the daughter of old *Leir,*
Who did unkindly difinherit thee:
But think thou art the noble *Gallian* queene,
And wife to him that dearely loveth thee:
Embrace the joyes that prefent with thee dwell,
Let forrow packe and hide herfelfe in hell.

Cordella.

Not that I miffe my country or my kinne,
My old acquaintance or my ancient friends,
Doth any whit diftemperate my mind,
Knowing you, which are more deare to me
Then country, kin, and all things els can be.

Yet

Yet pardon me, my gracious lord, in this:
For what can ſtop the courſe of nature's power?
As eaſy is it for foure-footed beaſts,
To ſtay themſelves upon the liquid aire,
And mount aloft into the element,
And overſtrip the feathered fowles in flight:
As eaſy is it for the ſlimy fiſh,
To live and thrive without the helpe of water:
As eaſy is it for the blackamoore,
To waſh the tawny colour from his ſkin,
Which all oppoſe againſt the courſe of nature:
As I am able to forget my father.

      King.
Myrrour of vertue, *Phœnix* of our age!
Too kind a daughter for an unkind father,
Be of good comfort; for I will diſpatch
Ambaſſadors immediately for *Brittaine*,
Unto the king of *Cornwall's* court, whereas
Your father keepeth now his reſidence,
And in the kindeſt maner him intreat,
That, ſetting former grievances apart,
He will be pleaſde to come and viſit us.
If no intreaty will ſuffice the turne,
Ile offer him the halfe of all my crowne:
If that moves not, weele furniſh out a fleet,
And ſaile to *Cornwall* for to viſit him;
And there you ſhall be firmely reconcilde
In perfit love, as earſt you were before.

      Cordella.
Where toung cannot ſufficient thanks afford,
The king of heaven remunerate my lord.

      King.
Only be blithe, and frolick (ſweet) with me:
This and much more Ile do to comfort thee.

    Enter Meſſenger ſolus.

     Meſſenger.
It is a world to ſee now I am fluſh,
How many friends I purchaſe every where!

          How

How many feekes to creepe into my favour,
And kiffe their hands, and bend their knees to me!
No more, here comes the queene, now fhall I know her mind,
And hope for to derive more crownes from her.

Enter Ragan.

Ragan.

My friend, I fee thou mind'ft thy promife well,
And art before me here, me thinks, to day.

Meffenger.

I am a poore man, and it like your grace;
But yet I alwayes love to keepe my word.

Ragan.

Wel, keepe thy word with me, and thou fhalt fee,
That of a poore man I will make thee rich.

Meffenger.

I long to heare it, it might have bin difpatcht,
If you had told me of it yefternight.

Ragan.

It is a thing of right ftrange confequence,
And well I cannot utter it in words.

Meffenger.

It is more ftrange, that I am not by this
Befide myfelfe, with longing for to heare it.
Were it to meet the devil in his denne,
And try a bout with him for a fcratcht face,
Ide undertake it, if you would but bid me.

Ragan.

Ah, good my friend, that I fhould have thee do
Is fuch a thing, as I do fhame to fpeake;
Yet it muft needs be done.

Meffenger.

Ile fpeake it for thee, queene: fhall I kill thy father?
I know 'tis that; and if it be fo, fay.

Ragan.

I.

Meffenger.

Why, that's ynough.

Ragan.

And yet that is not all.

Meffenger.

Meffenger.

What elfe ?

Ragan.

Thou muft kill that old man that came with him.

Meffenger.

Here are two hands, for eche of them is one.

Ragan.

And for eche hand here is a recompence.

                                  [Gives him two purfes.

Meffenger.

Oh, that I had ten hands by miracle !
I could teare ten in pieces with my teeth,
So in my mouth yould put a purfe of gold.
But in what manner muft it be effected ?

Ragan.

To morrow morning ere the breake of day,
I by a wyle will fend them to the thicket,
That is about fome two miles from the court,
And promife them to meet them there myfelfe,
Becaufe I muft have private conference,
About fome news I have receiv'd from *Cornwall.*
This is ynough, I know, they will not faile,
And then be ready for to play thy part :
Which done, thou mayft right eafily efcape,
And no man once miftruft thee for the fact :
But yet, before thou profecute the act,
Shew him the letter, which my fifter fent,
There let him read his owne inditement firft,
And then proceed to execution :
But fee thou faint not ; for they will fpeake faire.

Meffenger.

Could he fpeak words as pleafing as the pipe
Of *Mercury*, which charm'd the hundred eyes
Of watchful *Argos*, and inforc'd him fleepe:
Yet here are words fo pleafing to my thoughts,   *[To the purfe.*
As quite fhall take away the found of his.   *[Exit.*

Ragan.

About it then, and when thou haft difpatcht,
Ile find a meanes to fend thee after him).   *[Exit.*

                                  Enter

Enter Cornwall *and* Gonorill.

Cornwall.

I wonder that the meffenger doth ftay,
Whom we difpatcht for *Cambria* fo long fince :
If that his anfwere do not pleafe us well,
And he do fhew good reafon for delay,
Ile teach him how to dally with his king,
And to detaine us in fuch long fufpence.

Gonorill.

My lord, I thinke the reafon may be this :
My father meanes to come along with him ;
And therefore 'tis his pleafure he fhall ftay,
For to attend upon him on the way.

Cornwall.

It may be fo, and therefore till I know
The truth thereof, I will fufpend my judgement.

Enter Servant.

Servant.

And't like your grace, there is an ambaffador
Arrived from *Gallia*, and craves admittance to your majefty.

Cornwall

From *Gallia?* what fhould his meffage
Hither import ? is not your father happely
Gone thither ? well, whatfoere it be,
Bid him come in, he fhall have audience.

Enter Ambaffador.

What newes from *Gallia?* fpeake, ambaffador.

Ambaffador.

The noble king and queene of *Gallia* firft falutes,
By me, their honourable father, my lord *Leir :*
Next, they commend them kindly to your graces,
As thofe whofe wellfare they intirely wifh.
Letters I have to deliver to my lord *Leir,*
And prefents too, if I might fpeake with him.

Gonorill.

If you might fpeak with him ? why, do you thinke,
We are afraid that you fhould fpeake with him ?

Ambaffador.

Ambaſſador.

Pardon me, madam ; for I thinke not ſo,
But ſay ſo only, 'cauſe he is not here.

Cornwall.

Indeed, my friend, upon ſome urgent cauſe,
He is at this time abſent from the court :.
But if a day or two you here repoſe,
'Tis very likely you ſhall have him here,
Or elſe have certaine notice where he is.

Gonorill.

Are not we worthy to receive your meſſage ?

Ambaſſador.

I had in charge to do it to himſelfe.

Gonorill.

It may be then 'twill not be done in haſte.   [*To herſelfe.*
How doth my ſiſter brooke the aire of *Fraunce?*

Ambaſſador.

Exceeding well, and never ſicke one houre,
Since firſt ſhe ſet her foot upon the ſhore.

Gonorill.

I am the more ſorry.

Ambaſſador.

I hope not ſo, madam.

Gonorill.

Didſt thou not ſay, that ſhe was ever ſicke,
Since the firſt houre that ſhe arrived there ?

Ambaſſador.

No, madam, I ſaid quite contrary.

Gonorill.

Then I miſtooke thee.

Cornwall.

Then ſhe is merry, if ſhe have her health.

Ambaſſador.

Oh no, her griefe exceeds, until the time
That ſhe be reconcil'd unto her father.

Gonorill.

God continue it.

Ambaſſador.

What, madam ?

Gonorill.

Gonorill.

Why, her health.

Ambaſſador.

Amen to that: but God releaſe her griefe,
And ſend her father in a better mind,
Then to continue alwayes ſo unkind.

Cornwall.

Ile be a mediator in her cauſe,
And ſeeke all meanes to expiat his wrath.

Ambaſſador.

Madam, I hope your grace will do the like.

Gonorill.

Should I be a meane to exaſperate his wrath
Againſt my ſiſter, whom I love ſo deare ? no, no.

Ambaſſador.

To expiate or mittigate his wrath :
For he hath miſconceived without a cauſe.

Gonorill.

O, I, what elſe ?

Ambaſſador.

'Tis pity it ſhould be ſo ; would it were otherwiſe.

Gonorill.

It were great pity it ſhould be otherwiſe.

Ambaſſador.

Then how, madam ?

Gonorill.

Then that they ſhould be reconcilde againe.

Ambaſſador.

It ſhewes you beare an honourable mind.

Gonorill.

It ſhewes thy underſtanding to be blind,
And that thou hadſt need of an interpreter :

                                [Speakes to herſelfe.

Well, I will know thy meſſage ere't be long,
And find a meane to croſſe it, if I can.

Cornwall.

Come in, my friend, and frolick in our court,
Till certaine notice of my father come.   *[Exeunt.*

                    Enter

Enter Leir *and* Perillus.

Perillus.

My lord, you are up to day before your houre,
'Tis newes to you to be abroad so rathe.

Leir.

'Tis newes indeed, I am so extreme heavy,
That I can scarcely keepe my eye-lids open.

Perillus.

And so am I, but I impute the cause
To rising sooner then we use to do.

Leir.

Hither my daughter meanes to come disguis'd:
Ile fit me downe, and read until she come.

    [*Pulls out a booke, and sits downe.*

Perillus.

Sheele not be long, I warrant you, my lord:
But say, a-couple of these they call good fellowes
Should step out of a hedge, and set upon us,
We were in good case for to answere them.

Leir.

'Twere not for us to stand upon our hands.

Perillus.

I feare, we scant should stand upon our legs.
But how should we do to defend ourselves?

Leir.

Even pray to God, to blesse us from their hands:
For fervent prayer much ill hap withstands.

Perillus.

Ile sit and pray with you for company;
Yet was I ne're so heavy in my life.   [*They fall both asleepe.*

Enter the Messenger, or murtherer, with two daggers in his hands.

Messenger.

Were it not a mad jest, if two or three of my profession
should meet me, and lay me downe in a ditch, and play robbe
thiefe with me, and perforce take my gold away from me,
whilest I act this stratagem, and by this meanes the gray beards
should escape? Faith, when I were at liberty againe, I would
    E e   make

make no more to do, but go to the next tree, and there hang
myfelfe. *[Sees them, and ſtarts.*
But ſtay, me thinks, my youthes are here already,
And with pure zeale have prayed themfelves aſleepe.
I thinke, they know to what intent they came,
And are provided for another world.
[He takes their bookes away.
Now could I ſtab them bravely, while they ſleepe,
And in a maner put them to no paine;
And doing ſo, I ſhewed them mighty friendſhip :
For feare of death is worfe then death itſelfe.
But that my fweet queene will'd me for to ſhew
This letter to them, ere I did the deed.
Maſſe, they begin to ſtirre : Ile ſtand aſide ;
So ſhall I come upon them unawares. *[They wake and rife.*

Leir.
I marvel, that my daughter ſtays ſo long.

Perillus.
I feare, we did miſtake the place, my lord.

Leir.
God graunt we do not miſcarry in the place :
I had a ſhort nap, but ſo full of dread,
As much amazeth me to think thereof.

Perillus.
Feare not, my lord, dreames are but fantaſies,
And ſlight imaginations of the braine.

Meſſenger.
Perfwade him ſo, but Ile make him and you
Confeſſe, that dreames do often prove too true.

Perillus.
I pray, my lord, what was the effect of it ?
I may go neere to geſſe what it pretends.

Meſſenger.
Leave that to me, I will expound the dreame.

Leir.
Me thought, my daughters, *Gonorill* and **Ragan,**
Stood both before me with ſuch grim aſpects,
Eche brandiſhing a faulchion in their hand,
Ready to lop a lymme off where it fell,
And in their other hands a naked poinyard,

Wherewith

Wherewith they ftabb'd me in a hundred places,
And to their thinking left me there for dead :
But then my youngeft daughter, fair *Cordella*,
Came with a boxe of balfome in her hand,
And powred it into my bleeding wounds ;
By whofe good means I was recovred well,
In perfit health, as earft I was before:
And with the feare of this I did awake,
And yet for feare my feeble joints do quake.

     Meffenger.
Ile make you quake for fomething prefently.
Stand, ftand.   [*They reele.*

     Leir.
We do, my friend, although with much ado:.

     Meffenger.
Deliver, deliver.

     Perillus.
Deliver us, good Lord, from fuch as he.

     Meffenger.
You fhould have prayed before, while it was time,
And then perhaps, you might have fcapt my hands :
But you, like faithful watch-men, fell afleepe,   .
The whilft I came and tooke your halberds from you.

         [*Shews their bookes.*
And now you want your weapons of defence,
How have you any hope to be delivered?   .
This comes, becaufe you have no better ftay,
But fall afleepe, when you fhould watch and pray.

     Leir.
My friend, thou feemft to be a proper man.

     Meffenger.
'Sblood, how the old flave clawes me by the elbow ?
He thinks, belike, to fcape by fcraping thus.

     Perillus.
And it may be are in fome need of money.

     Meffenger.
That to be falfe, behold my evidence.   [*Shewes his purfe.*

     Leir.
If that I have will do thee any good,
I give it thee, even with a right good will.   [*Takes it.*
        E e 2   *Perillus.*

Perillus.

Here, take mine too, and wifh with all my heart,
To do thee pleafure, it were twice as much.
      [*Takes his, and weighs them both in his hands.*
      Meffenger.

Ile none of them, they are too light for me.
      [*Puts them in his pocket.*

Leir.

Why then farewell : and if thou have occafion
In any thing, to ufe me to the queene,
'Tis like ynough that I can pleafure thee.   [*They proffer to goe.*

Meffenger.

Do you heare, do you heare, fir?
If I had occafion to ufe you to the queene,
Would you do one thing for me I fhould afke?

Leir.

I, any thing that lies within my power.
Here is my hand upon it, fo farewel.   [*Proffer to goe.*

Meffenger.

Heare you, fir, heare you? pray, a word with you.
Me thinks, a comely honeft ancient man
Should not diffemble with one for a vantage.
I know, when I fhall come to try this geare,
You will recant from all that you have faid.

Perillus.

Miftruft not him, but try him when thou wilt :
He is her father, therefore may do much.

Meffenger.

I know he is, and therefore meane to try him :
You are his friend too, I muft try you both.

Ambo.

Prithy do, prithy do.   [*Proffer to go out.*

Meffenger.

Stay grey-beards then, and prove men of your words :
The queene hath tied me by a folemne oth,
Here in this place to fee you both difpatcht :
Now for the fafegard of my confcience,
Do me the pleafure for to kill yourfelves :
So fhall you fave me labour for to do it,
And prove yourfelves true old men of your words.

4

And

And here I vow in fight of all the world,
I ne're will trouble you whilſt I live againe.
     Leir.
 Affright us not with terror, good my friend,
Nor ſtrike ſuch feare into our aged hearts.
Play not the cat, which dallieth with the mouſe;
And on a ſudden maketh her a prey:
But if thou art markt for the man of death
To me and to my *Damion*, tell me plaine,
That we may be prepared for the ſtroke,
And make ourſelves fit for the world to come.
     Meſſenger.
 I am the laſt of any mortal race,
That ere your eyes are likely to behold,
And hither ſent of purpoſe to this place,
To give a final period to your dayes,
Which are ſo wicked, and have lived ſo long,
That your owne children ſeeke to ſhort your life.
     Leir.
 Camſt thou from *France*, of purpoſe to do this?
     Meſſenger.
 From *France?* zoones, do I looke like a *Frenchman?*
Sure I have not mine owne face on; ſome body hath chang'd
faces with me, and I know not of it: but I am ſure, my apparel
is all *Engliſh.* Sirrah, what meaneſt thou to aſke that queſtion?
I could ſpoile the faſhion of this face for anger. A *French*
face!
     Leir.
 Becauſe my daughter, whom I have offended,
And at whoſe hands I have deſerv'd as ill,
As ever any father did of child,
Is queene of *Fraunce*, no thanks at all to me,
But unto God, who my injuſtice ſee.
If it be ſo, that ſhee doth ſeeke revenge,
As with good reaſon ſhe may juſtly do,
I will moſt willingly reſigne my life,
A ſacrifice to mittigate her ire:
I never will intreat thee to forgive,
Becauſe I am unworthy for to live.
    E e 3   Therefore

Therefore fpeake foone, and I will foone make fpeed;
Whether *Cordella* will'd thee do this deed ?
Meffenger.

As I am a perfit gentlean, thou fpeakft *French* to me:
I never heard *Cordellae's* name before,
Nor never was in *Frannce* in all my life :
I never knew thou hadft a daughter there,
To whom thou didft prove fo unkind a churle :
But thy owne toung declares that thou haft bin
A vile old wretch, and full of heinous fin.
Leir.

Ah, no, my friend, thou art deceived much :
For her except, whom I confeffe I wrongd,
Through doting frenzy, and o're-jelous love,
There lives not any under heavens bright eye,
That can convict me of impiety :
And therefore fure thou doft miftake the marke :
For I am in true peace with all the world.
Meffenger.

You are the fitter for the King of heaven :
And therefore, for to rid thee of fufpence,
Know thou, the queenes of *Cambria* and *Cornwall*,
Thy owne two daughters, *Gonorill* and *Ragan*,
Appointed me to'maffacre thee here.
Why wouldft thou then perfwade me, that thou art
In charity with all the world? but now
When thy owne iffue hold thee in fuch hate,
That they have hired me t'abbridge thy fate,
Oh, fy upon fuch vile diffembling breath,
That would deceive, even at the point of death.
Perillus.

Am I awake, or is it but a dreame ?
Meffenger.

Feare nothing, man, thou art but in a dreame,
And thou fhalt never wake until doomefday
By then, I hope, thou wilt have flept ynough
Leir.

Yet, gentle friend, graunt one thing ere I die.
Meffenger.

Ile graunt you any thing, except your lives.

Leir.

Leir.

Oh, but affure me by fome certaine token,
That my two daughters hired thee to this deed:
If I were once refolv'd of that, then I
Would wifh no longer life, but crave to die.

Meffenger.

That to be true, in fight of heaven I fweare.

Leir.

Sweare not by heaven, for feare of punifhment:
The heavens are guiltleffe of fuch hainous acts.

Meffenger.

I fweare by earth, the mother of us all.

Leir.

Sweare not by earth:·for fhe abhors to beare
Such baftards, as are murtherers of her fonnes.

Meffenger.

Why then, by hell, and all the devils I fweare.

Leir.

Sweare not by hell; for that ftands gaping wide,
To fwallow thee, and if thou do this deed.

[*Thunder and lightning.*

Meffenger.

I would that word were in his belly againe,
It hath frighted me even to the very heart;
This old man is fome ftrong magician:
His words have turnd my mind from this exploit.
Then neither heaven, earth, nor hell, be witneffe;
But let this paper witneffe for them all.

[*Shewes* Gonorill's *letter.*

Shall I relent, or fhall I profecute?
Shall I refolve, or were I beft recant?
I will not crack my credit with two queenes,
To whom I have already paft my word.
Oh, but my confcience for this act doth tell,
I get heaven's hate, earth's fcorne, and paines of hell.

[*They bleffe themfelves.*

Perillus.

Oh juft *Jehova,* whofe almighty power
·Doth governe all things in this fpacious world,

E e 4

How

How canſt thou ſuffer ſuch outrageous acts
To be committed without juſt revenge?
O viperous generation and accurſt,
To ſeeke his blood, whoſe blood did make them firſt!

Leir.

Ah, my true friend in all extremity,
Let us ſubmit us to the will of God:
Things paſt all fence, let us not ſeeke to know;
It is God's-will, and therefore muſt be ſo.
My friend, I am prepared for the ſtroke:
Strike when thou wilt, and I forgive thee here,
Even from the very bottome of my heart.

Meſſenger.

But I am not prepared for to ſtrike.

Leir.

Farewel, *Perillus,* even the trueſt friend,
That ever lived in adverſity:
The lateſt kindneſſe Ile requeſt of thee,
Is that thou go unto my daughter *Cordella,*
And carry her her father's lateſt bleſſing:
Withal deſire her, that ſhe will forgive me;
For I have wrong'd her without any cauſe.
Now, Lord, receive me, for I come to thee,
And die, I hope, in perfit charity.
Diſpatch, I pray thee, I have lived too long.

Meſſenger.

I, but you are unwiſe, to ſend an errand
By him that never meaneth to deliver it:
Why, he muſt go along with you to heaven:
It were not good you ſhould go all alone.

Leir.

No doubt, he ſhal, when by the courſe of nature,
He muſt ſurrender up his due to death:
But that time ſhall not come till God permit.

Meſſenger.

Nay, preſently, to beare you company.
I have a paſport for him in my pocket,
Already ſeal'd, and he muſt needs ride poſte.
[*Shews a bagge of money.*

Leir.

Leir.

The letter which I read, imports not fo,
It only toucheth me, no word of him.

Meſſenger.

I, but the queene commaunds it muſt be fo,
And I am paid for him, as well as you.

Perillus.

I, who have borne you company in life,
Moſt willingly will beare a ſhare in death.
It ſkilleth not for me, my friend, a whit,
Nor for a hundred ſuch as thou and I.

Meſſenger.

Mary, but it doth, ſir, by your leave; your good dayes are
paſt: though it bee no matter for you, 'tis a matter for me,
proper men are not fo rife.

Perillus.

Oh, but beware, how thou doſt lay thy hand
Upon the high anointed of the Lord:
O, be adviſed ere thou doſt begin:
Difpatch me ſtraight, but meddle not with him,

Leir.

Friend, thy commiſſion is to deale with me,
And I am he that hath deferved all:
The plot was laid to take away my life:
And here it is, I do intreat thee take it:
Yet for my fake, and as thou art a man,
Spare this my friend, that hither with me came:
I brought him forth, whereas he had not bin,
But for good will to beare me company.
He left his friends, his country, and his goods,
And came with me in moſt extremity.
Oh, if he ſhould miſcarry here and die,
Who is the cauſe of it, but only I?

Meſſenger.

Why that am I, let that ne're trouble thee.

Leir.

O no, 'tis I. O, had I now to give thee
The monarchy of all the ſpacious world
To ſave his life, I would beſtow it on thee:

But

But I have nothing but thefe teares and prayers,
And the fubmiffion of a bended knee.   [*Kneels.*
O, if all this to mercy move thy mind,
Spare him, in heaven thou fhalt like mercy find.

Meffenger.

I am as hard to be moved as another, and yet me thinks the
ftrength of their perfwafions ftirres me a little.

Perillus.

My friend, if feare of the almighty power
Have power to move thee, we have faid ynough:
But if thy mind be moveable with gold,
We have not prefently to give it thee:
Yet to thyfelfe thou mayft do greater good,
To keepe thy hands itill undefilde from blood:
For do but well confider with thyfelfe,
When thou haft finifht this outragcous act,
What horrour ftill will haunt thee for the deed:
Think this againe, that they which would incenfe
Thee for to be the butcher of their father,
When it is done, for feare it fhould be knowne,
Would make a meanes to rid thee from the world:
Oh, then art thou for ever tied in chaines
Of everlafting torments to indure,
Even in the hoteft hole of grifly hell,
Such paines, as never mortal young can tell.

    [*It thunders.   He quakes, and lets fall the dagger next to*
    Perillus.

Leir.

O, heavens be thanked, he will fpare my friend.
Now, when thou wilt, come make an end of me.

    [*He lets fall the other dagger,*
    Perillus.

Oh, happy fight! he meanes to fave my lord.
The king of heaven continue this good mind.

Leir.

Why ftayft thou to do execution?

Meffenger.

I am as wilful as you for your life:
I will not do it, now you do intreat me.

                                     Perillus.

Perillus.

Ah, now I fee thou haft fome fparke of grace.

Meffenger.

Befhrew you for it, you have put it in me:
The parlofeft old men, that ere I heard.
Well, to be flat, Ile not meddle with you:
Here I found you, and here Ile leave you:
If any afke you why the cafe fo ftand?
Say that your toungs were better then your hands.

[*Exit Meffenger.*

Perillus.

Farewel. If ever we together meet,
It fhall go hard, but I will thee regreet.
Courage, my lord, the worft is overpaft;
Let us give thanks to God, and hie us hence.

Leir.

Thou art deceived; for I am paft the beft,
And know not whither for to go from hence:
Death had bin better welcome unto me,
Then longer life to adde more mifery.

Perillus.

It were not good to returne from whence we came,
Unto your daughter *Ragan* back againe.
Now let us go to *France*, unto *Cordella*,
Your youngeft daughter, doubtleffe fhe will fuccour you.

Leir.

Oh, how can I perfwade myfelfe of that,
Since the other two are quite devoy'd of love;
To whom I was fo kind, as that my gifts,
Might make them love me, if 'twere nothing elfe?

Perillus.

No worldly gifts, but grace from God on hie,
Doth nourifh vertue and true charity.
Remember well what words *Cordella* fpake,
What time you afkt her, how fhe lov'd your grace.
She faid, her love unto you was as much,
As ought a child to beare unto her father.

Leir.

But fhe did find, my love was not to her,
As fhould a father beare unto a child.

6   *Perillus.*

Perillus.

That makes not her love to be any leſſe,
If ſhe do love you as a child ſhould do:
You have tried two, try one more for my ſake,
Ile ne're intreat you further trial make.
Remember weil the dreame you had of late,
And thinke what comfort it foretels to us.

Leir.

Come, trueſt friend, that ever man poſſeſt,
I know thou counſailſt all things for the beſt:
If this third daughter play a kinder part,
It comes of God, and not of my deſert.   [*Exeunt.*

Enter the Gallian *Ambaſſador ſolus.*

Ambaſſador.

There is of late newes come unto the court,
That old lord *Leir* remaines in *Cambria:*
Ile hie me thither preſently, to impart
My letters and my meſſage unto him.
I never was leſſe welcome to a place
In all my life-time, then I have bin hither,
Eſpecially unto the ſtately queene,
Who would not caſt one gracious looke on me,
But ſtill with lowring and ſuſpicious eyes,
Would take exceptions at each word I ſpake,
And faine ſhe would have undermined me,
To know what my ambaſſage did import.
But ſhe is like to hop without her hope,
And in this matter for to want her will,
Though (by report) ſheele hav't in all things elſe.
Well, I will poſte away for *Cambria:*
Within theſe few dayes I hope to be there.   [*Exit.*

Enter the king and queene of Gallia, *and* Mumford.

King.

By this, our father underſtands our mind,
And our kind greetings ſent to him of late:

Therefore

Therefore my mind prefageth ere't be long,
We fhall receive from *Brittayne* happy newes.

Cordella.

I feare my fifter will diffwade his mind ;
For fhe to me hath alwayes bin unkind.

King.

Feare not, my love, fince that we know the worft,
The laft meanes helpes, if that we miffe the firft :
If hee'le not come to *Gallia* unto us,
Then we will faile to *Brittayne* unto him.

Mumford.

Well, if I once fee *Brittayne* againe,
I have fworne, Ile ne're come home without my wench,
And Ile not be forfworne,
Ile rather never come home while I live.

Cordella.

Are you fure, *Mumford,* fhe is a maid ftill ?

Mumford.

Nay, Ile not fweare fhe is a maid, but fhe goes for one :
Ile take her at all adventures, if I can get her.

Cordella.

I, that's well put in.

Mumford.

Well put in ? nay, it was ill put in ; for had it
Bin as well put in, as ere I put in, in my dayes,
I would have made her follow me to *Fraunce.*

Cordella.

Nay, you'd have bin fo kind, as take her with you,
Or elfe, were I as fhe,
I would have bin fo loving, as Ide ftay behind you :
Yet I muft confeffe, you are a very proper man,
And able to make a wench do more then fhe would do.

Mumford.

Well, I have a payre of flops for the nonce,
Will hold all your mocks.

King.

Nay, we fee you have a hanfome hofe.

Cordella.

I, and of the neweft fafhion.

Mumford.

Mumford.

More bobs, more : put them in ſtill,
They'l ſerve inſtead of bumbaſt, yet put not in too many, leſt
the ſeames crack, and they fly out amongſt you againe : you
muſt not think to outface me ſo eaſly in my miſtris quarrel,
who if I ſee once againe, ten teame of horſes ſhall not draw
me away, till I have full and whole poſſeſſion.

King.

I, but one teame and a cart will ſerve the turne.

Cordella.

Not only for him, but alſo for his wench.

Mumford.

Well, you are two to one, Ile give you over :
And ſince I ſee you ſo pleaſantly diſpoſed,
Which indeed is but ſeldome ſeene, Ile claime
A promiſe of you, which you ſhall not deny me :
For promiſe is debt, and by this hand you promiſd it me.
Therefore you owe it me, and you ſhall pay it me,
Or Ile ſue you upon an action of unkindueſſe.

King.

Prithy, lord *Mumford*, what promiſe did I make thee ?

Mumford.

Faith, nothing but this,
That the next faire weather, which is very now,
You would go in progreſſe downe to the ſea ſide,
Which is very neere.

King.

Faith, in this motion I will join with thee,
And be a mediator to my queene.
Prithy, my love, let this match go forward,
My mind foretels, 'twill be a lucky voyage.

Cordella.

Entreaty needs not, where you may commaund,
So you be pleaſde, I am right well content :
Yet, as the ſea I much deſire to ſee ;
So am I moſt unwilling to be ſeene.

King.

Weele go diſguiſed, all unknowne to any.

Cordella.

Howſoever you make one, Ile make another.

Mumford.

Mumford.

And I the third : oh, I am over-joyed !
See what love is, which getteth with a word,
What all the world befides could ne're obtaine :
But what difguifes fhall we have, my lord ?

King.

Faith thus : my queene and I will be difguifde,
Like a plaine country couple, and you fhall be *Roger*
Our man, and wait upon us : or if you will,
You fhall go firft, and we will wait on you.

Mumford.

'Twere more then time ; this device is excellent :
Come let us about it.   [*Exeunt.*

Enter Cambria *and* Ragan, *with nobles.*

Cambria.

What ftrange mifchance or unexpected hap
Hath thus depriv'd us of our father's prefence ?
Can no man tell us what's become of him,
With whom we did converfe not two dayes fince ?
My lords, let every where light horfe be fent,
To fcoure about through all our regiment.
Difpatch a pofte immediately to *Cornwall*,
To fee if any newes be of him there ;
Myfelfe will make a ftrict inquiry here,
And all about our cities neere at hand,
Till certaine newes of his abode be brought.

Ragan.

All forrow is but counterfet to mine,
Whofe lips are almoft fealed up with griefe :
Mine is the fubftance, whilft they do but feeme
To weepe the leffe, which teares cannot redeeme.
O, ne're was heard fo ftrange a mifadventure,
A thing fo far beyond the reach of fence,
Since no man's reafon in the caufe can enter.
What hath remov'd my father thus from hence ?
O, I do feare fome charme or invocation
Of wicked fpirits, or infernal fiends,
Stird by *Cordella*, moves this innovation,
And brings my father timeleffe to his end.

But

But might I know, that the detefted witch
Were certain caufe of this uncertaine ill,
Myfelfe to *Fraunce* would go in fome difguife,
And with thefe nailes fcrarch out her hateful eyes:
For fince I am deprived of my father,
I loath my life, and wifh my death the rather.

Cambria.

The heavens are juft, and hate impiety,
And will (no doubt) reveale fuch hainous crimes:
Cenfure not any, till you know the right:
Let him be judge, that bringeth truth to light.

Ragan.

O, but my griefe, like to a fwelling tide,
Exceeds the bourds of common patience:
Nor can I moderate my toung fo much,
To conceale them, whom I hold in fufpect.

Cambria.

This matter fhall be fifted: if it be fhe,
A thoufand *Fraunces* fhall not harbour her.

Enter the Gallian *Ambaffador.*

Ambaffador.

All happineffe unto the *Cambrian* king.

Cambria.

Welcom, my friend, from whence is thy ambaffage?

Ambaffador.

I came from *Gallia,* unto *Cornwall* fent,
With letters to your honourable father,
Whom there not finding, as I did expect,
I was directed hither to repaire.

Ragan.

Frenchman, what is thy meffage to my father?

Ambaffador.

My letters, madam, will import the fame,
Which my commiffion is for to deliver.

Ragan.

In his abfence you may truft us with your letters.

Ambaffador.

I muft performe my charge in fuch a manner,
As I have ftrict commaundment from the king.

Ragan.

Ragan.

, There is good packing twixt your king and you;
You need not hither come to afke for him,
You know where he is better then ourfelves

Ambaſſador.

Madam, I hope, not far off.

Ragan.

Hath the young murdreſſe, your outragicus queene,
No meanes to colour her deteſted deeds,
In finiſhing my guiltleſſe fathers dayes,
(Becauſe he gave her nothing to her dowre)
But by the colour of a fain'd ambaſſage,
To fend him letters hither to our court?
Go carry them to them that fent them hither,
And bid them keepe their fcroules unto themfelves:
They cannot blind us with fuch flight excufe,
To fmother up fo monftrous vild abufe.
And were it not, it is 'gainft law of armes,
To offer violence to a meſſenger,
We would inflict fuch torments on thyfelfe,
As ſhould inforce thee to reveale the truth.

Ambaſſador.

Madam, your threats no whit apall my mind,
I know my confcience guiltleſſe of this act;
My king and queene, I dare be fworne, are free
From any thought of fuch impiety:
And therefore, madam, you have done them wrong,
And ill befeeming with a fifters love,
Who in meere duty tender him as much,
As ever you refpected him for dowre.
The king your hufband will not fay as much.

Cambria.

I will fufpend my judgement for a time,
Till more appearance give us further light:
Yet to be plaine, your comming doth inforce
A great fufpicion to our doubtful mind,
And that you do refemble, to be briefe,
Him that firſt robs, and then cries, ftop the theefe.

Ambaſſador.

Pray God fome neere you have not done the like.

F f

Ragan.

Hence, faucy mate, reply no more to us;   [*She ftrikes him.*
For law of armes fhall not protect thy toung.

Ambaffador.

Ne're was I offred fuch difcourtefy;
God and my king, I truft, ere it be long,
Will find a meane to remedy this wrong.   [*Exit Ambaffador.*

Ragan.

How fhall I live, to fuffer this difgrace,
At every bafe and vulgar peafants hands?
It ill befitteth my imperial ftate,
To be thus ufde, and no man take my part.   [*She weeps.*

Cambria.

What fhould I do? infringe the law of armes,
Were to my everlafting obloquy:
But I will take revenge upon his mafter,
Which fent him hither, to delude us thus.

Ragan.

Nay, if you put up this, be fure, ere long,
Now that my father thus is made away;
Sheele come and claime a third part of your crowne,
As due unto her by inheritance.

Cambria.

But I will prove her title to be nought
But fhame, and the reward of parricide;
And make her an example to the world,
For after-ages to admire her penance.
This will I do, as I am *Cambriaes* king,
Or lofe my life, to profecute revenge.
Come, firft let's learne what newes is of our father,
And then proceed, as beft occafion fits.   [*Exeunt.*

Enter Leir, Perillus, *and two mariners in fea-gownes and fea-caps.*

Perillus.

My honeft friends, we are afham'd to fhew
The great extremity of our prefent ftate.
In that at this time we are brought fo low,
That we want money for to pay our paffage.

The

The truth is fo, we met with fome good fellowes,
A little before we came aboord your fhip,
Which ftript us quite of all the coine we had,
And left us not a penny in our purfes :
Yet wanting mony, we will ufe the meane,
To fee you fatisfied to the uttermoft.   [*Lookes on* Leir.

Firſt Mariner.

Here's a good gown, 'twould become me paffing wel,
I fhould be fine in it.   [*Lookes on* Perillus.

Second Mariner.

Here's a good cloke, I marvel how I fhould look in it.

Leir.

Faith, had we others to fupply their roome,
Though ne're fo meane, you willingly fhould have them.

Firſt Mariner.

Do you heare, fir ? you looke like an honeft man;
Ile not ftand to do you a pleafure : here's a good ftrong motly
gaberdine, coft me xiiij. good fhillings at *Billinſgate*, give me
your gowne for it, and your cap for mine, and Ile forgive
your paffage.

Leir.

With al my heart, and xx. thanks.   [Leir *and he changeth.*

Second Mariner.

Do you heare, fir? you fhall have a better match then he,
becaufe you are my friend : here is a good fheep's ruffet fea-
gowne, will bide more ftreffe, I warrant you, then two of his ;
yes, for you feem to be an honeft gentleman, I am content to
change it for your cloke, and afke you nothing for your paffage more.   [*Pulls off* Perillus's *cloke.*

Perillus.

My owne I willingly would change with thee,
And think myfelfe indebted to thy kindneffe :
But would my friend might keepe his garment ftill.
My friend, Ile give thee this new dublet, if thou wilt
Reftore his gowne unto him back againe.

Firſt Mariner.

Nay, if I do, would I might ne're eate powderd beefe and
muftard more, nor drink can of good liquor whilft I live.
My friend, you have fmall reafon to feeke to hinder me of my
bargaine : but the beft is, a bargaine's a bargaine.

Leir.

Kind friend, it is much better as it is.   [Leir *to* Perillus.
For by this meanes we may efcape unknowne,
Till time and opportunity do fit.

Second Mariner.

Hark, hark, they are laying their heads together,
Theile repent them of their bargaine anon,
'Twere beft for us to go while we are well.

Firft Mariner.

God be with you, fir, for your paffage back againe,
Ile ufe you as unreafonable as another.

Leir.

I know thou wilt; but we hope to bring ready money
With us, when we come back againe.   [*Exeunt mariners.*
Were ever men in this extremity,
In a ftrange country, and devoyed of friends,
And not a penny for to helpe ourfelves?
Kind friend, what thinkft thou will become of us?

Perillus.

Be of good cheere, my lord, I have a dublet
Will yeeld us mony ynough to ferve our turnes,
Until we come unto your daughter's court:
And then, I hope, we fhall find friends ynough.

Leir.

Ah, kind *Perillus,* that is it I feare,
And makes me faint, or ever I come there.
Can kindneffe fpring out of ingratitude?
Or love be reapt, where hatred hath bin fowne?
Can henbane joine in league with Methridate?
Or fugar grow in wormwoods bitter ftalke?
It cannot be, they are too oppofite:
And fo am I to any kindneffe here.
I have throwne wormwood on the fugred youth,
And like to henbane poifoned the fount,
Whence flowed the Methridate of a childs good wil.
I, like an envious thorne, have prickt the heart,
And turnd fweet grapes, to fowre unrelifht flocs:
The caufeleffe ire of my refpectleffe breft,
Hath fowrd the fweet milk of dame natures paps:

My

My bitter words have gauld her hony thoughts,
And weeds of rancour chokt the flower of grace.
Then what remainder is of any hope,
But all our fortunes will go quite aflope?

Perillus.

Feare not, my lord, the perfit good indeed
Can never be corrupted by the bad:
A new frefh veffel ftill retaines the tafte
Of that which firft is powr'd into the fame:
And therfore, though you name yourfelfe the thorn,
The weed, the gall, the henbane, and the wormewood;
Yet fheele continue in her former ftate,
The hony, milke, grape, fugar, Methridate.

Leir.

Thou pleafing orator unto me in wo,
Ceafe to beguile me with thy hopeful fpeaches:
O joine with me, and thinke of nought but croffes,
And then weele one lament anothers loffes.

Perillus.

Why, fay the worft, the worft can be but death,
And death is better then for to defpaire:
Then hazzard death, which may convert to life;
Banifh defpaire, which brings a thoufand deathes.

Leir.

Orecome with thy ftrong arguments, I yeeld
To be directed by thee, as thou wilt:
As thou yeeldft comfort to my crazed thoughts,
Would I could yeeld the like unto thy body,
Which is full weake, I know, and ill apaid,
For want of frefh meat and due fuftenance. .

Perillus.

Alack, my lord, my heart doth bleed, to think
That you fhould be in fuch extremity.

Leir.

Come, let us go, and fee what God will fend;
When all meanes faile, he is the fureft friend.   [*Excunt.*

Enter the Gallian *king and queene, and* Mumford *with a basket, disguised like countrey folke.*

King.
This tedious journey all on foot, sweet love,
Cannot be pleasing to your tender joints,
Which ne're were used to these toilesome walks.

Cordella.
I never in my life tooke more delight
In any journey, then I do in this:
It did me good, when as we hapt to light
Amongst the merry crue of country folke,
To see what industry and paines they tooke,
To win them commendations 'mongst their friends,
Lord, how they labour to bestir themselves,
And in their quirks to go beyond the moone,
And so take on them with such antike fits,
That one would think they were beside their wits!
Come away, *Roger*, with your basket.

Mumford.
Soft, dame, here comes a couple of old youthes,
I must needs make myselfe fat with jesting at them.

Enter Leir *and* Perillus *very faintly.*

Cordella.
Nay, prithy do not, they do seeme to be
Men much o'regone with griefe and misery.
Let's stand aside, and harken what they say.

Leir.
Ah, my *Perillus*, now I see we both
Shall end our dayes in this unfruitful soile,
Oh, I do faint for want of sustenance:
And thou, I know, in little better case.
No gentle tree affords one taste of fruit,
To comfort us, until we meet with men:
No lucky path conducts our lucklesse steps
Unto a place where any comfort dwels.
Sweet rest betide unto our happy soules;
For here I see our bodies must have end.

Perillus.

Perillus.

Ah, my deare lord, how doth my heart lament,
To fee you brought to this extremity!
O, if you love me, as you do profeſſe,
Or ever thought well of me in my life ; [*He ſtrips up his arme.*
Feed on this fleſh, whoſe veines are not ſo dry,
But there is vertue left to comfort you.
O, feed on this, if this will do you good,
Ile ſmile for joy, to fee you ſuck my bloud.

Leir.

I am no Caniball, that I ſhould delight
To ſlake my hungry jawes with humane fleſh :
I am no devil, or ten times worſe then ſo,
To ſuck the bloud of ſuch a peereleſſe friend.
O, do not think that I reſpect my life
So dearely, as I do thy loyal love.
Ah, *Brittayne*, I ſhall never fee thee more,
That haſt unkindly baniſhed thy king:
And yet not thou doſt make me to complaine,
But they which were more neere to me then thou.

Cordella.

What do I heare ? this lamentable voice,
Me thinks, ere now I oftentimes have heard.

Leir.

Ah, *Gonorill*, was halfe my kingdome's gift
The cauſe that thou didſt ſeeke to have my life?
Ah, cruel *Ragan*, did I give thee all,
And all could not ſuffice without my bloud ?
Ah, poore *Cordella*, did I give thee nought,
Nor never ſhall be able for to give ?
O, let me warne all ages that inſueth,
How they truſt flattery, and reject the trueth.
Well, unkind girles, I here forgive you both,
Yet the juſt heavens will hardly do the like;
And onely crave forgiveneſſe at the end
Of good *Cordella*, and of thee, my friend;
Of God, whoſe majeſty I have offended,
By my tranſgreſſion many thouſand wayes :
Of her, deare heart, whom I for no occaſion
Turn'd out of all, through flatterers perſwaſion:

Of

Of thee, kind friend, who but for me, I know,
Hadit never come unto this place of wo.

Cordella.

Alack, that ever I should live to see
My noble father in this misery.

King,

Sweet love, reveale not what thou art as yet,
Until we know the ground of all this ill.

Cordella.

O, but some meat, some meat: do you not see,
How neere they are to death for want of food?

Perillus.

Lord, which didst help thy servants at their need,
Or now or never send us helpe with speed.
Oh comfort, comfort! yonder is a banquet,
And men and women, my lord: be of good cheare:
For I see comfort comming very neere.
O my lord, a banquet, and men and women!

Leir.

O, let kind pity mollify their hearts,
That they may helpe us in our great extreames.

Perillus.

God save you, friends; and if this blessed banquet
Affordeth any food or sustenance,
Even for his sake that saved us all from death,
Vouchsafe to save us from the gripe of famine.

[*She bringeth him to the table.*

Cordella.

Here, father, sit and eat; here sit and drink:
And would it were far better for your sakes!

[*Perillus takes Leir by the hand to the table.*

Perillus.

Ile give you thanks anon: my friend doth faint,
And needeth present comfort.   [*Leir drinkes.*

Mumford.

I warrant, he ne're stayes to say a grace:
O, there's no sauce to a good stomake.

Perillus.

The blessed God of heaven hath thought upon us.

Leir,

Leir.

The thanks be his, and these kind courteous folke,
By whose humanity we are preferved.

[*They eat hungerly*; Leir *drinkes.*

Cordella,

And may that draught be unto him, as was
That which old *Eson* dranke, which did renue
His withered age, and made him young againe.
And may that meat be unto him, as was
That which *Elias* ate, in strength whereof
He walked fourty dayes, and never fainted.
Shall I conceale me longer from my father?
Or shall I manifest myfelfe to him?

King.

Forbeare a while, until his strength returne,
Left being over-joyed with feeing thee,
His poore weake fences should forfake their office,
And fo our caufe of joy be turn'd to forrow.

Perillus.

What chere, my lord? how do you feele yourfelfe?

Leir.

Me thinks, I never ate fuch favory meat:
It is as pleafant as the blefled manna,
That rain'd from heaven amongft the *Ifraelites:*
It hath recall'd my fpirits home againe,
And made me frefh, as earft I was before.
But how shall we congratulate their kindneffe?

Perillus.

Infaith, I know not how fufficiently;
But the beft meane that I can think on, is this;
Ile offer them my dublet in requital;
For we have nothing elfe to fpare.

Leir.

Nay, ftay, *Perillus*, for they shall have mine.

Perillus.

Pardon, my lord, I fweare they shall have mine.

[Perillus *proffers his dublet: they will not take it.*

Leir.

Ah, who would think fuch kindnes should remaine
Among fuch ftrange and unacquainted men:

And

And that fuch hate fhould harbour in the breft
Of thofe, which have occafion to be beft?

Cordella.

Ah, good old father, tell to me thy griefe,
Ile forrow with thee, if not adde reliefe.

Leir.

Ah, good young daughter, I may call thee fo;
For thou art like a daughter I did owe.

Cordella.

Do you not owe her ftill? what, is fhe dead?

Leir.

No, God forbid: but all my intereft's gone,
By fhewing my felfe too much unnatural:
So have I loft the title of a father,
And may be call'd a ftranger to her rather.

Cordella.

Your title's good ftill: for tis alwayes knowne,
A man may do as him lift with his owne.
But have you but one daughter then in all?

Leir.

Yes, I have more by two, then would I had.

Cordella.

O, fay not fo, but rather fee the end;
They that are bad, may have the grace to mend:
But how have they offended you fo much?

Leir.

If from the firft I fhould relate the caufe,
'Twould make a heart of adamant to weepe;
And thou, poore foule, kind-hearted as thou art,
Doft weepe already, ere I do begin.

Cordella.

For Gods love tell it; and when you have done,
Ile tell the reafon why I weepe fo foone.

Leir.

Then know this firft, I am a *Brittaine* borne,
And had three daughters by one loving wife:
And though I fay it, of beauty they were fped;
Efpecially the youngeft of the three,
For her perfections hardly matcht could be:
On thefe I doted with a jelous love,

And

And thought to try which of them lov'd me beſt,
By aſking them, which would do moſt for me?
The firſt and ſecond flattred me with words,
And vowd they lov'd me better then their lives :
The youngeſt ſaid, ſhe loved me as a child
Might do : her anſwere I eſteem'd moſt vild,
And preſently in an outragious mood,
I turnd her from me to go ſinke or ſwim :
And all I had, even to the very clothes,
I gave in dowry with the other two :
And ſhe that beſt deſerv'd the greateſt ſhare,
I gave her nothing, but diſgrace and care.
Now mark the ſequel : when I had done thus,
I ſojournd in my eldeſt daughters houſe,
Where for a time I was intreated well,
And liv'd in ſtate ſufficing my content :
But every day her kindneſſe did grow cold,
Which I with patience put up well ynough,
And ſeemed not to ſee the things I ſaw :
But at the laſt ſhe grew ſo far incenſt
With moody fury, and with cauſleſſe hate,
That in moſt vild and contumelious termes,
She bade me pack, and harbour ſomewhere elſe.
Then was I faine for refuge to repaire
Unto my other daughter for reliefe ;
Who gave me pleaſing and moſt courteous words ;
But in her actions ſhewed her ſelfe ſo ſore,
As never any daughter did before :
She prayd me in a morning out betime,
To go to a thicket two miles from the court,
Pointing that there ſhe would come talke with me :
There ſhe had ſet a ſhag haird murdring wretch,
To maſſacre my honeſt friend and me.
Then judge your ſelfe, although my tale be briefe,
If ever man had greater cauſe of griefe.

King.

Nor never like impiety was done,
Since the creation of the world begun.

Leir.

Leir.

And now I am conftraind to feeke reliefe
Of her, to whom I have bin fo unkind;
Whofe cenfure, if it do award me death,
I muft confefle fhe payes me but my due:
But if fhe fhew a loving daughters part,
It comes of God and her, not my defert.

Cordella.

No doubt fhe will, I dare be fworne fhe will.

Leir.

How know you that, not knowing what fhe is?

Cordella.

Myfelfe a father have a great way hence,
Ufde me as ill as ever you did her;
Yet, that his reverend age I once might fee,
Ice creepe along, to meet him on my knee.

Leir.

O, no mens children are unkind but mine.

Cordella.

Condemne not all, becaufe of others crime:
But looke, deare father, looke, behold and fee
Thy loving daughter fpeaketh unto thee.   [*She kneeles.*

Leir.

O, ftand thou up. it is my part to kneele,
And afke forgivenefle for my former faults.   [*He kneeles.*

Cordella.

O, if you wifh I fhould injoy my breath,
Deare father rife, or I receive my death.   [*He rifeth.*

Leir.

Then I will rife, to fatisfy your mind,
But kneele againe, til pardon be refignd.   [*He kneeles.*

Cordella.

I pardon you: the word befcomes not me:
But I do fay fo, for to eafe your knee;
You gave me life, you were the caufe that I
Am what I am, who elfe had never bin.

Leir.

But you gave life to me and to my friend,
Whofe dayes had elfe had an untimely end.

Cordella.

Cordella.

You brought me up, when as I was but young,
And far unable for to helpe myfelfe.

Leir.

I caft thee forth, when as thou waft but young,
And far unable for to helpe thyfelfe.

Cordella.

God, world, and nature, fay I do you wrong,
That can indure to fee you kneele fo long.

King.

Let me breake off this loving controverfy,
Which doth rejoice my very foule to fee.
Good father, rife, fhe is your loving daughter,   [*He rifeth.*
And honours you with as refpective duty,
As if you were the monarch of the world.

Cordella.

But I will never rife from off my knee,   [*She kneeles.*
Until I have your blelfing, and your pardon
Of all my faults committed any way,
From my firft birth unto this prefent day.

Leir.

The blelfing, which the God of *Abraham* gave
Unto the tribe of *Juda*, light on thee,
And multiply thy dayes, that thou mayft fee
Thy childrens children profper after thee.
Thy faults, which are juft none that I do know,
God pardon on high, and I forgive below.   [*She rifeth.*

Cordella.

Now is my heart at quiet, and doth leape
Within my breft, for joy of this good hap:
And now (deare father) welcome to our court,
And welcome (kind *Perillus*) unto me,
Mirrour of vertue and true honefty.

Leir.

O, he hath bin the kindeft friend to me,
That ever man had in adverfity.

Perillus.

My toung doth faile, to fay what heart doth think,
I am fo ravifht with exceeding joy.

King.

King.

All you have fpoke: now let me fpeak my mind,
And in few words much matter here conclude: [*He kneeles.*
If ere my heart do harbour any joy,
Or true content repofe within my breft,
Till I have rooted out this viperous fect,
And repofleft my father of his crowne,
Let me be counted for the perjurdft man,
That ever fpake word fince the world began.   [*Rifes.*

Mumford.

Let me pray to, that never pray'd before ;
                           [Mumford *kneeles.*
If ere I refalute the *Brittifh* earth,
(As (ere't be long) I do prefume I fhall)
And do returne from thence without my wench,
Let me be gelded for my recompence.   [*Rifes.*

King.

Come, let's to armes for to redreffe this wrong :
Till I am there, me thinks the time feemes long.   [*Exeunt.*

Enter Ragan *fola.*

Ragan.

I feele a hell of confcience in my breft,
Tormenting me with horrour for my fact,
And makes me in an agony of doubt,
For feare the world fhould find my dealing out.
The flave whom I appointed for the act,
I ne're fet eye upon the peafant fince :
O, could I get him for to make him fure,
My doubts would ceafe, and I fhould reft fecure.
But if the old men, with perfwafive words,
Have fav'd their lives, and made him to relent ;
Then are they fled unto the court of *Fraunce,*
And like a trumpet manifeft my fhame.
A fhame on thefe white-liverd flaves, fay I,
That with faire words fo foone are overcome.
O God, that I had bin but made a man ;
Or that my ftrength were equal with my will !
Thefe foolifh men are nothing but meere pity,

                                         And

And melt as butter doth againſt the ſun.
Why ſhould they have pre-eminence over us,
Since we are creatures of more brave reſolve?
I ſweare, I am quite out of charity
With all the heartleſſe men in *Chriſtendome*.
A poxe upon them, when they are affraid
To give a ſtab, or ſlit a paltry wind-pipe,
Which are ſo eaſy matters to be done.
Well, had I thought the ſlave would ſerve me ſo,
Myſelfe would have bin executioner:
Tis now undone, and if that it be knowne,
Ile make as good ſhift as I can for one.
He that repines at me, how ere it ſtands,
'Twere beſt for him to keepe him from my hands.   [*Exit.*

Sound drums and trumpets: Enter the Gallian *king,* Leir,
Mumford, *and the army.*

King.

Thus have we brought our army to the ſea,
Whereas our ſhips are ready to receive us:
The wind ſtands faire, and we in foure houres ſaile,
May eaſily arrive on *Brittiſh* ſhore,
Where unexpected we may them ſurpriſe,
And gaine a glorious victory with eaſe.
Wherefore, my loving countreymen, reſolve,
Since truth and juſtice fighteth on our ſides,
That we ſhall march with conqueſt where we go.
Myſelf will be as forward as the firſt,
And ſtep by ſtep march with the hardieſt wight:
And not the meaneſt ſouldier in our campe
Shall be in danger, but Ile ſecond him.
To you, my lord, we give the whole command
Of all the army, next unto ourſelfe;
Not doubting of you, but you will extend
Your wonted valour in this needful caſe,
Encouraging the reſt to do the like,
By your approved magnanimity.

Mumford.

My liege, tis needleſſe to ſpur a willing horſe,
Thats apt enough to run himſelfe to death:

3

For here I sweare by that sweet saints bright eye,
Which are the starres, which guide me to good hap,
Either to see my old lord crownd anew,
Or in his cause to bid the world adieu.

Leir.

Thanks, good lord *Mumford*, tis more of your good will,
Then any merit or desert in me.

Mumford.

And now to you, my worthy countreymen,
Ye valiant race of *Genonsian Gawles*,
Surnamed *Red-shanks*, for your chivalry,
Because you fight up to the shanks in bloud ;
Shew yourselves now to be right *Gawles* indeed,
And be so bitter on your enemies,
That they may say, you are as bitter as gall.
Gall them, brave shot, with your artillery :
Gall them, brave halberts, with your sharp point billes,
Each in their pointed place, not one, but all,
Fight for the credit of yourselves and *Gawle*.

King.

Then what should more perswasion need to those,
That rather wish to deale, then heare or blowes ?
Let's to our ships, and if that God permit,
In foure houres sail, I hope we shall be there.

Mumford.

And in five houres more, I make no doubt,
But we shall bring our wish'd desires about.   [*Exeunt.*

Enter a Captaine of the Watch, and two Watchmen.

Captaine.

My honest friends, it is your turne to night,
To watch in this place, neere about the beacon,
And vigilantly have regard,
If any fleet of ships passe hitherward :
Which if you do, your office is to fire
The beacon presently, and raise the towne.   [*Exit.*

First Watchman.

I, I, I; feare nothing ; we know our charge, I warrant : I
have bin a watchman about this beacon this xxx. yere, and
yet I ne're see it stir, but stood as quietly as might be.

Second

Second Watchman.

Faith neighbour, and you'l follow my vice, infead of watching the beacon, wee'l go to goodman *Gennings,* and watch a pot of ale and a rafher of bacon : and if we do not crink ourfelves drunke, then fo ; I warrant, the beacon will fee us when we come out againe.

Firf Watchman.

I, but how if fome body excufe us to the captaine ?

Second Watchman.

Tis no matter, Ile prove by good reafon that we watch the beacon : affe for example.

Firf Watchman.

I hope you do not call me affe by craft, neighbour.

Second Watchman.

No, no, but for example : fay here ftands the pot of ale, thats the beacon.

Firf Watchman.

I, I, tis a very good beacon.

Second Watchman.

Well, fay here ftands your nofe, thats the fire.

Firf Watchman.

Indeed I muft confeffe, tis fomewhat red.

Second Watchman.

I fee come marching in a dith, halfe a fcore pieces of falt bacon.

Firf Watchman.

I underftand your meaning, thats as much to fay, half a fcore fhips.

Second Watchman.

True, you confter right ; prefently, like a faithful watch-man, I fire the beacon, and call up the towne.

Firf Watchman.

I, thats as much as to fay, you fet your nofe to the pot, and drink up the drink.

Second Watchman.

You are in the right ; come, let's go fire the beacon.

[*Exeunt.*

G g   :   *Enter*

Enter the king of Gallia *with a still march,* Mumford *and soldiers.*

King.

Now march our enfignes on the *Brittifh* earth,
And we are neere approching to the towne :
Then looke about you, valiant countrymen,
And we fhall finifh this exploit with eafe.
Th' inhabitants of this miftruftful place
Are dead afleep, as men that are fecure :
Here fhall we fkirmifh but with naked men,
Devoid of fence, new waked from a dreame,
That know not what our comming doth pretend,
Till they do feele our meaning on their fkinnes :
Therefore affaile : God and our right for us.   [*Exeunt.*

Alarm, with men and women halfe naked : Enter two Captaines without dublets, with fwords.

Firft Captain.

Where are thefe villaines that were fet to watch,
And fire the beacon, if occafion ferv'd,
That thus have fuffred us to be furprifde,
And never given notice to the towne ?
We are betray'd, and quite devoid of hope,
By any meanes to fortify ourfelves.

Second Captain.

Tis ten to one the peafants are o'recome with drinke and fleep, and fo neglect their charge.

Firft Captaine.

A whirl-wind carry them quick to a whirl-poole,
That there the flaves may drinke their bellies full.

Second Captaine.

This tis, to have the beacon fo neere the ale-houfe.

Enter the Watchmen drunke, with each a pot.

Firft Captaine.

Out on ye, villaines, whither run you now ?

Firft Watchman.

To fire the towne, and call up the beacon.

Second Watchman.

No, no, fir, to fire the beacon.   [*He drinkes.*
                                            Second.

Second Captaine.

What, with a pot of ale, you drunken rogues ?

First Captain.

You'l fire the beacon, when the towne is loft :
Ile teach you how to tend your office better.

[*Draws to ftab them.*

Enter Mumford, *Captaines run away.*

Mumford.

Yeeld, yeeld, yeeld.   [*He kicks downe their pots.*

First Watchman.

Reele ? no, we do not reele :
You may lacke a pot of ale ere you die.

Mumford.

But in meane fpace, I anfwer, you want none.
Wel, there; no dealing with you, y'are tall men, and wel
 weapond ;
I would there were no worfe then you in the towne.   [*Exit.*

Second Watchman.

A fpeaks like an honeft man, my cholers paft already.
Come, neighbour, let's go.

First Watchman.

Nay, firft let's fee and we can ftand.   [*Exeunt.*

[*Alarum, excurfions,* Mumford *after them, and fome halfe naked.*

Enter the Gallian *king,* Leir, Mumford, Cordella, Perillus, *and
 fouldiers, with the chiefe of the towne bound.*

King.

Feare not, my friends, you fhall receive no hurt,
If you'l fubfcribe unto your lawful king,
And quite revoke your fealty from *Cambria,*
And from afpiring *Cornwall* too, whofe wives
Have practifde treafon 'gainft their fathers life.
Wee come in juftice of your wronged king,
And do intend no harme at all to you,
So you fubmit unto your lawful king.

Leir.

Kind countrymen, it grieves me, that perforce,
I am conftrain'd to ufe extremities.

G g 2   *Nobles.*

Nobles.

Long have you here bin lookt for, good my lord,
And wifh'd for by a general confent :
And had we known your highneffe had arrived,
We had not made refiftance to your grace :
And now, my gracious lord, you need not doubt,
But all the country will yeeld prefently,
Which fince your abfence have bin greatly tax'd,
For to maintaine their overfwelling pride.
Weele prefently fend word to all our friends ;
When they have notice, they will come apace.

Leir.

Thanks, loving fubjects ; and thanks, worthy fon,
Thanks, my kind daughter, thanks to you, my lord,
Who willingly adventured have your blood,
(Without defert) to do me fo much good.

Mumford.

O, fay not fo :
I have bin much beholding to your grace :
I muft confeffe, I have bin in fome fkirmifhes,
But I was never in the like to this :
For where I was wont to meet with armed men,
I was now incountred with naked women.

Cordella.

We that are feeble, and want ufe of armes,
Will pray to God, to fheeld you from all harmes.

Leir.

The while your hands do manage ceafeleffe toile,
Our hearts fhall pray, the foes may have the foile.

Perillus.

Weeie faft and pray, whilft you for us do fight,
That victory may profecute the right.

King.

Me thinks, your words do amplify (my friends)
And adde frefh vigor to my willing limmes :   [*Drum.*
But harke, I heare the adverfe drum approach.
God and our right, faint *Denis*, and faint *George.*

I

Enter

Enter Cornwall, Cambria, Gonorill, Ragan, *and the army.*

Cornwall.

Prefumptuous king of *Gawles*, how dareft thou
Prefume to enter on our *Brittijh* fhore ?
And more then that, to take our townes perforce,
And draw our fubjects hearts from their true king ?
Be fure to buy it at as deare a price,
As ere you bought prefumption in your lives.

King.

Ore-daring *Cornwall*, know, we came in right,
And juft revengement of the wronged king,
Whofe daughters thefe, fell vipers as they are,
Have fought to murder and deprive of life :
But God protected him from all their fpight,
And we are come in juftice of his right.

Cambria.

Nor he nor thou have any intereft here,
But what you win and purchafe with the fword.
Thy flaunders to our noble vertuous queenes,
Wee'l in the battel thruft them down thy throte,
Except for feare of our revenging hands,
Thou flye to fea, as not fecure on lands.

Mumford.

Welfhman, Ile fo ferrit you ere night for that word,
That you fhall have no mind to crake fo wel this twelvemonth.

Gonorill.

They lye, that fay, we fought our father's death.

Ragan.

'Tis meerely forged for a colour's fake,
To fet a glofle on your invafion.
Me thinks, an old man ready for to die,
Snould be afham'd to broache fo foule a lie.

Cordella.

Fy, fhamelefle fifter, fo devoyed of grace,
To call our father lier to his face.

Gonorill.

Peace (puritan) diffembling hypocrite,
Which art fo good, that thou wilt prove ftark naught :

Anon,

Anon, when as I have you in my fingers,
Ile make you wifh yourfelfe in purgatory.

Perillus.

Nay, peace thou monfter, fhame unto thy fexe:
Thou fiend in likeneffe of a humane creature.

Ragan.

I never heard a fouler fpoken man.

Leir.

Out on thee, viper, fcum, filthy parricide,
More odious to my fight then is a toade:
Knoweft thou thefe letters?   [*She fnatches them and teares them.*

Ragan.

Think you to outface me with your paltry fcrowles?
You come to drive my hufband from his right,
Under the colour of a forged letter.

Leir.

Who ever heard the like impiety?

Perillus.

You are our debtour of more patience:
We were more patient when we ftaid for you,
Within the thicket two long houres and more.

Ragan.

What houres? what thicket?

Perillus.

There, where you fent your fervant with your letters,
Seal'd with your hand, to fend us both to heaven,
Where, as I thinke, you never meane to come.

Ragan.

Alas, you are growne a child againe with age,
Or elfe your fences dote for want of fleepe.

Perillus.

Indeed you made us rife betimes, you know,
Yet had a care we fhould fleepe where you bade us ftay,
But never wake more till the latter day.

Gonorill.

Peace, peace, old fellow, thou art fleepy ftill.

Mumford.

Faith, and if you reafon till to morrow,
You get no other anfwere at their hands.

'Tis

'Tis pitty two such good faces
Should have so little grace betweene them.
Well, let us see if their husbands with their hands
Can do as much as they do with their toungs.

Cambria.

I, with their swords they'l make your toung unsay
What they have said, or else they'l cut them out.

King.

Too't, gallants, too't, let's not stand brawling thus.

                         [Exeunt both armies.

Sound Alarum: excursions. Mumford *must chase* Cambria *away:*
        then cease. Enter Cornwall.

Cornwall.

The day is lost, our friends do all revolt,
And joine against us with the adverse part :
There is no meanes of safety but by flight,
And therefore Ile to *Cornwall* with my queene.   *[Exit.*

Enter Cambria.

Cambria.

I thinke, there is a devil in the campe hath haunted me to
day : he hath so tired me, that in a maner I can fight no
more.

Enter Mumford.

Zounds ! here he comes, Ile take me to my horse.   *[Exit.*
       [Mumford *followes him to the dore, and returnes.*
              Mumford.

Farewel *(Welshman)* give thee but thy due,
Thou hast a light and nimble paire of legs :
Thou art more in debt to them then to thy hands :
But if I meet thee once againe to day,
Ile cut them off, and set them to a better heart.   *[Exit.*

Alarums and excursions, then sound victory. Enter Leir,
    Perillus, King, Cordella, *and* Mumford.

King.

Thanks be to God, your foes are overcome,
And you againe possessed of your right.

                                 Leir.

Leir.

Firſt to the heavens; next, thanks to you, my ſonne,
By whoſe good meanes I repoſſeſſe the ſame :
Which if it pleaſe you to accept yourſelf,
With all my heart I will reſigne to you :
For it is yours by right, and none of mine.
Firſt, have you raiſd, at your owne charge, a power
Of valiant ſouldiers (this comes all from you) ;
Next have you ventured your owne perſons ſcathe.
And laſtly (worthy *Gallia* never ſtaind),
My kingly title I by thee have gaind.

King.

Thank heavens, not me, my zeale to you is ſuch,
Commaund my utmoſt, I will never grutch.

Cordella.

He that with all kind love intreats his queene,
Will not be to her father unkind ſeene.

Leir.

Ah, my *Cordella*, now I call to mind,
The modeſt anſwere, which I tooke unkind :
But now I ſee, I am no whit beguild,
Thou lovedſt me dearly, and as ought a child.
And thou *(Perillus)* partner once in woe,
Thee to requite, the beſt I can, I'le doe :
Yet all I can, I, were it ne're ſo much,
Were not ſufficient, thy true love is ſuch.
Thanks (worthy *Mumford)* to thee laſt of all,
Not greeted laſt, 'cauſe thy deſert was ſmall ;
No, thou haſt lion-like laid on to day,
Chaſing the *Cornwall* king and *Cambria*;
Who with my daughters, daughters did I ſay ?
To ſave their lives, the fugitives did play.
Come, ſonne and daughter, who bid me advaunce,
Repoſe with me a while, and then for *Fraunce*.

[*Sound drumes and trumpets.* *Exeunt.*

F I N I S.

www.ingramcontent.com/pod-product-compliance
Lightning Source LLC
Chambersburg PA
CBHW030556040726
47497CB00008B/2757